POISON
IN
PARADISE

Melissa Baldwin

To my author tribe! Our Friday night zoom calls made social distancing more bearable.

BOOKS BY MELISSA BALDWIN

On the Road to Love

Sailing into Love
(short story in the Pushing Up Daisies Collection)

Friends ForNever

Poison in Paradise

Acknowledgements:

To my publisher Gemma Halliday, thank you for your example and for taking another chance on me and my stories.

To my awesome editors Wendi Baker and Susie Halliday, thank you for your advice and encouragement, and especially for cleaning up after me.

To my wonderful readers! Thank you for your support. I hope that my stories continue to bring joy to your lives.

CHAPTER ONE

————

Another sailing, another group of lovely passengers aboard our grand vessel, the *Legend,* the jewel of the Epic Cruise Line. We'd been at sea for approximately an hour, the tropical drinks were flowing, the guests were going crazy charging lavish amounts to their staterooms, and one of the pools had already been closed due to an impromptu cleaning. A few of our adorable younger guests had decided to throw their ice cream cones into the water. As a lifeguard, the all-you-can-eat cold dessert wasn't my favorite perk of our ship, but the guests loved it.

With the sun shining in the distance and sounds of reggae music played on steel drums filling the air, we were officially on our way to the first port of call in the Caribbean and ready to enjoy four fun-filled nights aboard our fantastic ship. As I sat on my lifeguard chair overlooking the large pool, I thought about how lucky I was. I, Alexa Walker, was getting paid to sail on the open ocean and soak up vitamin D. My brown hair was pulled up into a high ponytail, popping out of the top of my *Epic Cruise Line* sun visor, and my uniform was a comfortable dry-fit T-shirt and shorts.

I loved my job.

Someday I would write a book about my adventures with Epic Cruise Line, but for the moment I'd stick to planning memories for our guests that would last a lifetime. And, of course, saving lives.

I had wanted to be a lifeguard since the day I'd been saved by a blond-haired, blue-eyed surfer boy named Ian off Florida's east coast. It had been the summer I turned fifteen, and I'd spent most of it at the beach with my parents. I loved being in the ocean so much I'd even taken a few surfing lessons. I remember paddling out, full of confidence, until a strong rip current had pulled me under the water. The feeling of sheer helplessness had washed over me faster than the wave, and panic had set in. I'd been sure I was going to die until a pair of strong arms lifted my head above the water and dragged me to shore. I'd never forget how grateful I'd been in that moment, and I'd wanted to be a lifeguard ever since.

However, after being lucky enough to work as a lifeguard with the Epic Cruise Line for the last two years, I was ready to expand my résumé beyond the pool. I still loved saving lives, but part of me had started to notice that the other lifeguards were all in their early twenties. And I was in my…let's just say slightly older than that by only a few years. So, when a part-time position with Port Adventures opened, I jumped on it. And checking out the exciting points of interest in each town we docked in for myself was an added bonus. I'd been doing double duty on board for a few months now, lifeguarding and working with our Port Adventures team. The two positions kept me busy, but I loved them both.

Believe it or not there was just as much action planning adventures for our guests as there was watching over the pool waters. I was surprised to find that discussing a fun-filled excursion could cause so much strife within a family. Weren't vacations supposed to be all about togetherness? Who knew that choosing between an experience with dolphins or turtles could cause a knock-down, drag-out fight? This had actually happened on my last sailing. The argument had been between sisters-in-law who'd brought their personal issues on the ship with them. Their husbands had had to pull them apart because making the decision had led up to an actual physical altercation. Luckily, I'd saved the day by suggesting they do both excursions. It was a simple resolution, but I think they'd just wanted a reason to fight. It had been entertaining to say the least.

I did one last scan of the pool before the end of my shift—so far, so good.

As soon as Steven came to relieve me, I quickly ran to my stateroom to get changed. When I arrived, my roommate, Chloe, was there, adding soft, beachy waves to her hair.

"How was your shift, Lexi?"

"Have I told you how much I hate ice cream?" I asked as I opened my closet and grabbed my favorite pale blue shift dress. "And whose idea was it to put self-serve machines on this ship?"

"Let me guess… Children were playing in it," she said with a laugh.

"Worse. They threw their cones into the pool."

She cringed. "Another reason I don't want children. They are much too messy."

I turned on the shower and tested the water.

"Oh, come on. I'm sure you and Levi would have some gorgeous children together, and they would have the cutest accents." I loved when little kids spoke with accents. Chloe was originally from Norway, but her home was in London when she wasn't sailing.

She was a stunning blonde-haired, blue-eyed beauty. Her latest boyfriend—or, as she called him, "friend who is a boy"—Levi was from the Netherlands, and his eyes were even more blue than hers. I felt a bit plain next to her, with my golden-brown hair, hazel eyes, and Floridian accent (according to Chloe). *Do Floridians have an accent?* I didn't think so.

"My *friend* Levi and I haven't had any discussion about children," she insisted. "What about you? Have you met any of the new transfers yet?"

Chloe was a hopeless romantic, and the fact I hadn't had a love interest in a very long time drove her mad (her words). Several new crew members had joined our ship over the past week, and she thought I should check them out.

"Not yet. I've been busy *working*," I replied.

She rolled her eyes. "Well, hop to it. I've heard there are some good options."

I quickly jumped into the shower to avoid any more discussion of potential onboard love affairs. It wasn't that I wasn't curious about the new staff members—it was just that I had a job to do. But after working on the ship for months at a time, it was good to get some fresh blood in here.

* * *

As I glanced out the round porthole window next to my desk, I caught a glimpse of the sun fading into the horizon. That view never got old. The Port Adventures office was located on Deck Four, right next to the shopping area. Our department had one of the best locations on the ship because it was right in the middle of the action. Guests wouldn't be able to miss us on their way to purchase all the duty-free goodies and Epic Cruise Line souvenirs. The office was cozy, with dark wood desks and soft navy blue chairs. Our office walls were covered with paintings of the different landscapes of our ports of call, which had proven to be a great selling point. It was a nice change of scenery from being on higher decks and out in the sun all day.

I opened my schedule and scrolled through the list. My first guests of the evening were Phillip and Josie Edwards. As I read through their profile, I was shocked to see they were from my hometown, Winter Park, Florida.

"Hello. We have an appointment at six thirty," a voice called. I looked up to see a muscular man holding a rocks glass filled with brown liquid, with a petite blonde peeking around behind him.

"Come in, Mr. and Mrs. Edwards," I said, standing up to greet them. "I'm Alexa Walker. I'll be helping you select your activities."

"Lexi Walker, is that you?" the woman interrupted as soon as she sat down.

All of a sudden I realized she looked very familiar.

"Josie Brooks?"

When she smiled, I immediately knew it was her. Holy crap, my best friend from fourth grade was here on my ship. It'd been years since I last saw her. Obviously she looked older, and I could tell she'd had some work done. Her cheekbones were higher, and her lips were fuller.

"It's Josie Edwards now," she said, placing her martini glass down before shoving her left hand in my face. The diamond on her ring finger looked much too big for her tiny hand.

"I can't believe it," she exclaimed. "I haven't seen you since we were kids."

"What happened to you?" I asked. "The last thing I remember was Mr. Stanley telling the class that you had moved."

She nodded. "My parents had a messy divorce, and my mom basically wanted us to start a whole new life. She sent me to a private school, and I lost touch with all my friends. It was the saddest time of my life."

I knew the feeling. I remembered crying to my mom about Josie moving away.

"This is such an amazing coincidence," Josie exclaimed, flipping her long blonde hair over her shoulder. She was wearing the shortest white dress I'd ever seen, and it fit her like a glove. "Baby, isn't this so funny? Lexi and I were best friends in elementary school."

Josie's husband, Phillip, didn't seem amused about the interesting twist of fate. He quickly drained his glass and placed it down on my desk.

"Yes, it's great," he said as he stared at the pages of the Port Adventures brochure like it was the most interesting thing he'd ever read. Clearly he didn't want to engage in our small talk about our past friendship. "So, we want to book the ultimate full-day experience at Paradise Island tomorrow."

"We're meeting up with some people who are already staying at the resort. It's a belated wedding celebration with some good friends," Josie added.

I smiled as I entered their information into my computer. "Okay, the ultimate will include private transportation to and from the ship, luxury cabanas, private servers, poolside massages, and entertainment. Would you like a cost breakdown? You can remove any of the—"

"Those are all fine," he interrupted. "And go ahead and sign us up for the stingray experience the day after tomorrow," Phillip said, still not looking up from the brochure. Judging by his silence during Josie's and my conversation, I could tell Phillip was a no-nonsense kind of guy. From what I could tell, Josie had most of the personality in their relationship.

"Sounds good, right, Josie?" he added finally.

Josie took a sip of her bright pink cocktail. "Sure. I told you I'd be happy with anything. Us being together is all that matters to me."

He leaned over and gave her a quick kiss on the cheek.

Typical newlywed couple—they both still thought the other one walked on water. Or at least they wanted it to look like they did. I had witnessed that behavior many times—blissful newlyweds who would do anything to please each other. They made a cute couple though. Josie was just as adorable and tiny as I remembered her, and Phillip reminded me of a big teddy bear. But only in stature—he seemed more aloof than warm.

"Your profile says you're traveling with another couple?" I asked, scrolling through my computer screen. "Will they be joining you tomorrow?"

"Oh yes, those are our best friends, Bobby and Michelle," Josie said. "Bobby and Phil have known each other since before they could walk. Right, babe?"

"Yep," Phillip agreed, still not looking up.

As I continued to enter their information into my computer, Josie and I chatted about Winter Park.

"It's been so long since I've been to Park Avenue," I told her. "Is the Briar Patch Restaurant still there? My family would go there almost every Sunday for breakfast."

"It sure is," she exclaimed. "It's one of my favorites, too. We have brunch there at least once a month."

It was nice to reminisce about my old stomping grounds, even though it made me a little homesick. I hadn't been to Central Florida since right before transferring to the ship. Even when we'd sailed out of the nearby ports, I hadn't had time to visit between debarkation and embarkation. My parents had moved to Tampa a few years before I got the job with Epic Cruise Line, so I'd visited them during my time off.

"How long have you been working here?" she asked.

Although it'd been years since I'd seen Josie, she seemed the same in a lot of ways—outgoing and bubbly. Everyone had wanted to be friends with her in elementary school.

"I've been on this ship for about seven months, but I've worked for the cruise line for two years. I absolutely love it here. It's a great company."

Josie drained her glass. "Wow, two years? That seems like a long time. You do get some time off, right?"

I laughed. "Of course I do."

A look of relief came over her face. I wondered if she actually believed I didn't get days off. Although, it wasn't that many.

"Good to know. It seems like everyone works really hard to keep these ships running smoothly."

I beamed. It was nice to know some people appreciated the time our staff put in to make memorable vacations for our guests.

"Okay, you're all set with your plans for the next two days. I'll be stopping by the resort sometime tomorrow to check in with my contact there." I handed her my card. "Feel free to reach out to me if you have any issues or questions. I'm happy to make any changes for you—that's why I'm here. And it was great seeing you again, Josie."

"Thank you," Phillip said, already on his feet. He was making his way toward the door when Josie grabbed his arm.

"Hang on!" she shouted. She stopped her husband and whispered something in his ear. I watched curiously as he looked back at me and shrugged his shoulders.

"Whatever you want," he said with a sigh.

Josie turned toward me and put her arms out.

"Lexi, I'd love to catch up some more. You should come join us at the pool tomorrow. You'll be at the resort anyway, right? Why don't you stop by and have a drink or some food?"

Wait, what?

I gave her a grateful smile. "Oh. That's very sweet, and I definitely appreciate the offer, but I'll be working, and my roommate will probably be with me because she has the day off."

One of the best things about Chloe being a performer on board was that she had most of her days free when we were docked in port. She could go to the beach, lounge at the pool, shop, or do basically anything she wanted unless she had a special show or event.

"Bring her along," she exclaimed. "We're meeting up with a few friends and Phillip's brother. It'll be a lot of fun, and most of them are from Central Florida. You may even know someone."

Hmm…I doubted that. I hadn't lived in Winter Park in over two years, and most of my good friends had moved away.

"I really should check with Chloe," I hesitated.

I wasn't sure how she'd feel about spending her day off with some random guests, although it wouldn't have been the first time. There had been the time she'd met those Australian soccer players—although she'd made me promise not to bring them up anymore.

"Can you call her now?"

I looked at the time. Chloe would already be into her first set. I shook my head. "She's working. She's one of the ship's musicians and won't be off until tonight."

Josie frowned. I had a feeling she was used to getting her way, which didn't surprise me.

"Why don't you leave a message in our stateroom after you talk to her? You're welcome to swing by if you have a chance," Phillip suggested as he eyed his empty glass. It was obvious he wanted to move on, perhaps to the casino or the bar.

I forced a smile. "I could, but are you sure? I wouldn't want to impose on your celebration."

"It's fine," Phillip insisted. I could sense the irritation in his voice. "Like my mother always says, the more the merrier."

I couldn't help but notice Josie's expression change at the mention of his mother. Judging by her slight cringe, I'd have guessed she wasn't a fan of her new in-law.

Phillip reached for his wife's arm and led her toward the door.

"Oh, I really hope you can make it. I'm so happy to see you again," Josie called.

After they left, I couldn't help but think about Josie's offer. Unlike Chloe, I'd never been invited to celebrate with our guests before.

It probably wouldn't be a big deal to briefly stop by. *Right?* And it *was* my job to make sure all activities in port were running smoothly.

I poked my head out my door to where my coworker Trina was sitting. "How's it going?"

She gave me a thumbs-up. "I just booked a Jet Ski experience for a family of five."

"That's awesome."

I sat back down at my desk to get ready for my next appointment, and a few minutes later there was a loud knock on my door. I sat up straight and plastered a smile on my face, ready to greet our next guests.

"Come on in! Welcome to Port Adventures."

The door opened, but it wasn't the Wilson family that I'd been expecting. I sucked in a breath as I drank in the stranger standing in my doorway. I immediately noticed his green eyes, sandy brown hair, and defined, strong jawline. He was wearing a light blue shirt, and the top few buttons were undone, showing a tad bit of his broad chest. I forced myself to lift my gaze up from the way it clung to his pectorals. Judging by the size of his chest and arms, it looked like the guy did at least a thousand push-ups a day.

"Oh, hi," I said absently. I quickly checked my schedule. Had I forgotten to add another meeting to my calendar?

"Hello. Do you have a few minutes?" he asked, his voice laced with a sexy British accent.

I stood up from my chair and semi-casually smoothed down my skirt.

"Sure. I was just waiting on my next guests. How can I help you?"

He approached my desk and held out his hand.

"I'm Jack Carson, the new director of marketing and public relations for the cruise line," he said.

Jack Carson was here? Okay, so he was like my boss's boss's boss, or something like that. And from what I'd heard, he had a reputation—a reputation of being extremely driven and very successful in the cruise industry. I'd also heard he was super-hot, and obviously I could see that for myself. I had plenty of friends on other ships, and we regularly communicated with each other. It was interesting to actually meet him in person. And he had a sexy British accent, which was always a bonus.

"Oh, it's nice to meet you, Mr. Carson."

"You can call me Jack," he replied politely.

"Um, okay. I'm Alexa Walker, but you can call me Lexi," I said playfully.

Ugh. I sounded so stupid. Everyone called me Lexi. Now was not the time to act silly or flirtatious. I needed to be professional.

He raised his eyebrow and gave me a nod. "It's good to meet you. I'll be working on board for the next few months. I'm hoping to make positive changes similar to those made on the other ships in our line—our reviews across all the travel websites are the best in the industry. The ratings have skyrocketed, and I plan to do the same thing here."

"Yes, of course," I agreed. "I'll do whatever I can to help."

A good first impression was very important. I was already a team player. Now I had to show Jack Carson.

He made himself comfortable in the chair across from my desk, and I returned to my seat.

"You've only been in this department a few months, isn't that right?"

I sat up straighter. "Yes, but I feel my time and knowledge of our cruise line made it an easy transition. I love working with our guests in every capacity."

"You're also a lifeguard."

I couldn't tell if he was impressed or not. He was very hard to read.

"Yes. I've been certified for years, and I'm committed to making sure our guests are safe. When this position opened, I thought it would be a great chance to help in other ways, like making their vacations unforgettable. After two years of sailing, I'm very familiar with our ports of call."

I needed to slow down because I'd started rambling. One corner of Jack's mouth curled up into a half smile. I noticed his lips were full, and behind them his teeth were perfectly straight and white.

"Alright, well, the strategy I've implemented is putting together strong teams of staff members who've gone above and beyond in their roles, and it's been very successful. It's my job to ensure we maintain the great reputation of our fleet."

I nodded eagerly. "Absolutely."

"I've spent most of today making the rounds, checking in with different departments, and so far I've seen a lot of potential," he continued. "I think there's a stellar group on board, and perhaps some of those staff members could excel in other roles on the ship. My success rate is proven—I'm sure you've seen articles on *FaveTripTips.com*, *On the Water Times*, and *Vacation Sensation* magazine."

Other roles? I hope he didn't plan on making too many changes. As much as I loved being a lifeguard, I enjoyed my new position.

"And how are you getting on so far this sailing?" he asked as he flashed me a brilliant smile.

The rumors were true. Jack Carson was gorgeous.

"Great. I just met with a lovely newlywed couple."

Lovely? Crap, I sounded like my grandmother. She wasn't British, but she used the word *lovely* and called everyone darling. Perhaps listening to his accent was rubbing off on me?

"What I mean is, the couple I met with is from my hometown, and they're very nice. Coincidentally, I went to elementary school with the wife. I booked two full days of activities for them while we're in the Bahamas," I said proudly.

It was the perfect opportunity to show him I was an asset to the Port Adventures Department. And in an effort to cover up the fact that I'd called the newlyweds lovely, I wanted to tell him about their invitation. "The couple, Josie and Phillip Edwards, invited me to stop by their party while I'm at the resort. I'm not sure I'll be able to, but I usually check in with my contacts there to ensure they're prepared to give our guests the best service possible. This is the first time a guest has invited me to stop by though. I'd say that's a win for our team."

He gave me a thoughtful look. "You could pop in to ensure they are receiving proper Epic Cruise Line treatment. I think it'd be good PR for us. And interacting with our guests is an important part of your job. Remember, one of our main goals is to make sure they return to sail with us again. We don't want them going to our competition."

I caught myself staring again. He had thick brown hair, and for a second I wondered what it'd be like to run my fingers through it. *Gah! What was wrong with me?* He was my boss— and therefore he was off-limits. It was still difficult not to stare, despite my worry that he could fire me at any moment. Okay, so maybe I was being dramatic, but it was possible. He could very well find his own people and move them into this department.

"I know," I replied. I almost reminded him that I'd been working with Epic for two years, but I stopped myself. "I'll be there anyway, so why not?"

"Exactly," he said knowingly. "Although, I'm not sure I should trust a Miami Dolphins fan to do the job."

I opened my mouth in shock. "Excuse me?"

He pointed to the picture on my desk of me wearing a Dolphins sweatshirt. My father had been a diehard fan for as long as I could remember, and it had carried on to the next generation in our family.

"What does that mean?" I asked. I could feel my blood pressure rise. My dad had taught us to defend our team no matter what.

He held his hands up in defense. "Isn't it obvious? Everyone knows the Patriots are the best team in football."

I rolled my eyes. Although I knew the team was really good, I wasn't going to give him the satisfaction of agreeing with him.

"Of course you'd say that. There are so many bandwagon fans out there. Do they even follow American football in the UK?"

I didn't know if I was crossing a line with him, but he'd started it.

He laughed for the first time since entering my office. "To answer your question, I've lived all over the world and followed the sport for many years. The Dolphins are less than favorable most of the time."

"Oh, really?" I snapped. "We'll see what happens next season. And much like my favorite team, you'll find I have a very strong work ethic."

Wasn't that why he was here anyway? What did football have to do with PR for the cruise line or the Port Adventures Department?

An amused smile spread across his face. "I look forward to seeing your work ethic in action. I'll be in touch to follow up on our guests' experiences. I'm hoping they have good things to say about their day. Have a *lovely* evening, Ms. Walker."

He was gone before I had a chance to respond. Our conversation ended rather formally. I guess *Jack* didn't feel comfortable calling me Lexi, and was he teasing me with his *lovely* comment?

I sat back down in my chair and thought about our interaction. Jack was here to do his job, but I couldn't help but be intrigued by his possible flirtation. At least it seemed like he was flirting by teasing me about my football team. Truthfully, I was rusty in that area.

My next guests arrived before I could think about Jack any longer. There was a family with four children waiting for me to help them plan their adventures, and that was more important. If Jack was planning on making changes in my department, it was time for me to shine.

One thing was for sure, I needed to check in on Josie and her crew tomorrow. I was now dead set on making sure the Edwards would return to Epic Cruise Line. Jack would see that this Dolphins fan was an asset to this company, if it was the last thing I'd ever do.

CHAPTER TWO

———

Working for a cruise line gave me the opportunity to learn a lot about how people vacationed. I'd met guests from all walks of life in my years with Epic. My favorites were the first-time cruisers. Most of them had worked and saved for years to sail on a grand ship like ours. Witnessing their excitement about being on board and visiting different locations around the world was what had really made me want to work in the Port Adventures Department. Then there were the seasoned vacationers and families who took trips once or twice a year. Many of them already knew what to expect but still looked forward to new experiences. And lastly the guests like Josie and Phillip and their friends who probably traveled often. Phillip knew which activities he wanted to do, and money didn't seem to be an issue. He seemed very familiar with the Bahamas.

To my surprise Chloe was happy to join me in port, even though I was technically working. She'd tagged along every once in a while in between her rehearsals to take in the tropical islands. I let Josie know we'd be stopping by and reminded her to contact me with any concerns about their transportation or itinerary.

Our first stop at the resort was to check in with my contact, Ty. I loved working with him, and his office reminded me of something you'd see on the *Golden Girls*. It was bright and open, the walls were a pale pink color, and there were potted palm trees in every corner.

"I'm so proud of you for making friends with the guests," Ty teased.

I liked Ty a lot. He was shorter than me by about two inches, making him about 5'5". When I first met him, he'd told me that the best people came in small packages, and in his case, he was right.

"How many times have I suggested you grab a drink and chill at the pool while you're here?" he asked.

Chloe snorted.

"What?" I asked with a scowl.

She shrugged. "He's right. You can take a break for a few minutes. I think it'll do you some good. Perhaps you'll even meet a dashing stranger."

I thought about Jack Carson's arrival. There was no way I'd be vacationing while on the job unless he was aware of it first. I ignored Chloe's suggestion.

"Anyway, can you make sure to tell the staff to take extra good care of the Edwards?"

Ty smiled. "Don't we always look after your guests? Epic Cruise Line is our favorite."

I rolled my eyes. "Oh honey, you say that to all the cruise lines."

"I do. But I really mean it this time," he said with a wink.

We all laughed, and then Chloe and I excused ourselves to catch up with Josie and her crew.

As we walked outside, I smiled. Sometimes I wanted to pinch myself that it was really my job to visit so many exotic travel destinations. Some people waited their whole lives to see different places in the world, and I got to experience it every day. We couldn't have asked for better weather. The sun was beaming through a few fluffy white clouds, and the sky was a brilliant shade of blue. There was a subtle breeze that moved the branches of the palm trees just a bit. The salty smell of the Atlantic Ocean filled the air, and I was eager to hear how our guests were enjoying this port of call.

The Paradise Island Resort was massive, with five separate pool areas and various amenities, including hot tubs, bars, and a lazy river. Chloe and I found the pool where the Edwards and their party were celebrating. There was a DJ playing some soothing reggae music, which set the mood for the perfect island experience. I was pleased to see that they were taking full advantage of the private cabanas, dedicated servers waiting to bring them something off the menu, and unlimited alcohol. I wanted them to return to the ship and rave about the day I'd planned for them.

I couldn't help but notice that everyone in their group was beautiful. The women were tanned and fit, and the men didn't look like they'd missed many workouts either.

Of course Josie and Phillip had extra treatment, including poolside massage, due to their arrangements made by *moi*, courtesy of the Epic Cruise Line.

"Lexi, I'm so happy you could stop by," Josie said. She was wearing a tiny yellow bikini, the biggest sunglasses I'd ever seen, and she had a delicate gold chain adorning her waist.

"Thank you. How was the transportation over here?"

I decided I should remain in work mode as much as possible, especially if anyone decided to check up behind me, and by "anyone" I meant Jack Carson. Ever since our brief meeting the night before, I wondered if he'd be watching me. Not in a creepy way, but he'd made his plans for the *Legend* very clear.

"The transportation was excellent. Even Phillip was impressed with the service we've received. He has very high expectations, so good job."

I felt a sense of relief. It was a good start. Hopefully the day continued to go smoothly.

"Michelle, Bobby, come here," she called.

Josie began to introduce Chloe and me to their friends.

"Bobby is Phil's oldest friend, and Michelle is his girlfriend."

Michelle looked like she just fell out of a Victoria's Secret catalog, her wavy auburn hair cascading down her back. I wondered if that was her natural color, because it was gorgeous. Bobby was so tall, he towered over the rest of us. He had dark brown hair and a slender build. We exchanged hellos, and Bobby paused when he met Chloe. This was a common occurrence because Chloe was stunning, with her sparkling blue eyes and perfect smile, but seriously, his also gorgeous girlfriend was standing right there.

"So, you're the girls who work on the cruise ship?" he asked, not taking his eyes off Chloe.

Chloe pretended to be interested in something on her phone, not that I blamed her because it was awkward with his girlfriend standing right there.

I flashed him a big smile. "We are. I work with the Port Adventures team on Epic Cruise Line."

"Oh yeah? So you're in charge of the fun stuff? Sounds like a good gig."

I shrugged. "You could say that. I help our guests book excursions and activities while the ship is docked. One of our main goals is to make sure our guests are satisfied and happy so they'll return to sail with us again. I told Josie I was coming over here today, and she was kind enough to invite me to stop by. When our guests make requests, we go above and beyond for them."

Okay, that sounded kind of cheesy but very convincing. Jack was clear about following up on our guest experiences, so I was going to be as over-the-top as I had to be.

Josie smiled. "Of course I did. You're one of my oldest friends. Lexi and I went to elementary school together. Isn't that funny? We were best friends in fourth grade, and somehow we ended up on the same cruise ship after all these years."

Bobby took a sip of his beer. "Really? It's a small world after all. So, Lexi, you plan activities for cruise line guests?"

"Yes, and I'm a lifeguard."

He raised his eyebrows. "That's good to know—in case anyone here needs to be saved." He paused. "You never know what can happen with this crazy group."

I looked around. Everyone seemed pretty calm so far. There were a couple people chatting on the steps of the pool, and a few were sitting around the tiki bar. Maybe the party was just getting started? There were only about eight people that I could see. I was glad it turned out to be a more intimate setting. Thankfully with so many pools on the property, the hotel guests were able to spread out.

"And what do you do, Chloe?" Bobby asked.

I glanced at Michelle, who was typing something on her phone. She seemed oblivious to her boyfriend's blatant interest in

Chloe, and maybe she didn't care. Regardless, there was an awkward vibe coming from them. They could be one of those couples with an open relationship. Not that it mattered. It was none of my business.

"I'm with the entertainment staff. I'm one of the musicians on the ship."

"You're a performer?" Bobby asked. "Very impressive. What exactly do you do?"

"I play piano and sing a little."

"She's fantastic," I added. "Our cruise line is well known in the industry for our entertainment. We've won several awards."

It didn't hurt to mention some of our accolades.

Bobby gave her a flirtatious smile. "Really? Well, I look forward to catching your show while I'm on board."

"Come and meet everyone else," Josie exclaimed, grabbing both of our hands.

Chloe and I happily followed her. I heard Bobby say something about catching up later, which I would try to avoid. He was friendly, but it bothered me the way he acted in front of his girlfriend.

"This is Phillip's older brother Drew," Josie said fondly.

Drew looked exactly like Phillip, except a little taller with less hair. And he seemed a lot friendlier.

"Welcome, ladies. Glad you could join us."

"Thanks," I said.

Drew offered to get us drinks, a sparkling water for me and a fruity cocktail for Chloe. Unlike her, I was still working, so no alcohol for me. As Drew headed to the bar, Josie continued with the introductions.

Within a few minutes we were introduced to the other guests, and I knew I'd never remember all their names.

"Let's get this party started for our new married friend," a girl with wavy pink hair yelled. She grabbed Josie's arm and pulled her toward a DJ. Hip-hop music suddenly filled the air, and Josie began bouncing to the beat.

"This is my bride tribe," Josie yelled. "Make yourselves comfortable."

Drew returned with our drinks. "So, what's it like working on a cruise ship?"

Chloe and I looked at each other and smiled.

"It's rather amazing," she answered.

"I love it," I added.

He folded his arms and gazed off toward the dance floor, where most of the guests had gathered. "I can't imagine what it'd be like to wake up every morning on the ocean."

"It's awesome, most of the time," I told him. "And we at Epic Cruise Line are committed to making sure our guests have the most unforgettable experience. We hope Josie and Phillip enjoy their vacation."

"It looks like it's off to a great start," Drew said before he excused himself.

Chloe and I found a table near the bar and sat down. I looked at my phone to check for any missed messages.

"So, this is interesting," she said, removing the piece of pineapple from the side of her glass.

I shrugged as I looked around. "You certainly have a fan in Bobby."

She rolled her eyes. "Yes, well, no thank you."

I giggled. "That was really awkward, but the girlfriend didn't seem to care, so why should we?"

"Yes, I'm guessing it's not the first time he hit on a woman in front of her," Chloe said. "I know his type."

I snorted. "You don't even know him."

"And you don't know Josie either," she insisted. "It's practically been a lifetime since you saw her."

"This group can be a lot to take," a voice said.

I turned around to see a short blonde girl with a messy bun on the top of her head. We'd met her a few minutes before, but of course I'd already forgotten her name.

"I'm Kelsey," she reminded us, holding up her glass.

"Why aren't you out there with the girls?" Chloe asked. We all looked at Josie, who was dancing with three girls, including Bobby's girlfriend.

Kelsey took a sip of her drink as she eyed the women cheering from the dance floor. "Because I'm not a part of Josie's bride tribe."

I detected some bitterness in her voice.

Chloe gave me a side glance. It was obvious to both of us that there was a good story to go along with Kelsey's admission.

"Sounds to me like you may have quite a tale to tell," Chloe declared with a wicked gleam in her eye. She lived for this kind of stuff and was always the first to find out the good gossip on the ship. I was a little surprised she hadn't heard Jack was joining us, not that she had an in with upper management. Most of the stuff she found out was about our coworkers' personal lives. When were people going to learn that nothing was a secret when you worked and lived together 24-7?

Kelsey pulled a chair over to join us. "I wouldn't call it a tale. I grew up with Phil and Bobby. The three of us were inseparable when we were kids, and our parents are all still best friends. They vacation and spend holidays together. We're basically one big happy family—well, sometimes."

So Kelsey was Phillip's friend, not Josie's. That explained her comment about not being a part of the tribe. I couldn't tell if it bothered her or not.

"Anyway, you know how it is. With our families being so close, the guys are kind of stuck with me," she said with a forced laugh.

Chloe leaned in closer to her. "So, be honest, is everyone here really as nice as they seem, or is it just an act?"

I kicked Chloe under the table. She might have been off the clock, but we were still representing the cruise line. As I expected, she continued to ignore me.

"So why didn't everyone just come on the cruise?" I asked, trying to deflect from Chloe's question.

Kelsey shrugged. "At first Josie and Phillip were going on the cruise alone and everyone was meeting down here in the Islands. But then they ended up inviting Bobby and Michelle to join them."

She stared in Josie's direction and then threw back what was left in her glass. "They didn't invite the rest of us."

I scanned the crowd and watched as Josie and her tribe danced together while Chloe continued asking Kelsey questions.

"Are you having a good time so far?"

"Sure," Kelsey said. She stretched her arms up over her head. "It'd be hard not to enjoy a resort like this."

"It's so cool that you all came down here to celebrate your friends' marriage," Chloe said. "Josie is so nice."

Kelsey nodded. "Mmhmm…"

Judging by her aloof reaction, I could tell she wasn't a Josie fan.

"To be honest, we were all surprised when they got married," Kelsey added. She lowered her voice. "They only dated for about eight months, and she wasn't the type of girl the Edwards envisioned as their daughter-in-law."

What did she mean by that?

"Excuse me, ladies," Phillip interrupted. He drained the remaining liquid in his glass. "Kelsey, can I speak to you privately?"

He was even more cold than he'd been the night before.

Hmm… I wondered if he'd overheard what Kelsey had said about his marriage.

She stood up. "It was nice talking to you."

I watched as she followed Phillip away from the pool area.

"Okay, I bet there's something going on between those two. I know romantic tension when I see it."

I raised my eyebrows. "What? He just got married to Josie."

"Oh yes. And it's obvious Kelsey isn't Josie's biggest fan," Chloe whispered. "Maybe she's jealous that Phillip married her instead."

I laughed. "You love any kind of potential drama, don't you?"

She held up her glass. "Hey, you dragged me here. Can't I have some fun?"

"I didn't *drag* you here."

"That's the story I'm sticking with," she said with a shrug.

I shook my head and stared off in the direction Phillip and Kelsey had gone. I had to agree with one thing Chloe said. Kelsey didn't like Josie, and she was doing a terrible job trying to hide her feelings. For some reason, I wondered what she and

Phillip were talking about. Josie was still on the dance floor with her bride tribe.

Chloe and the bartender started discussing the resort, so I excused myself to go to the restroom. As soon as I walked through the door, I was hit with the scents of lavender and eucalyptus. It smelled like a day spa, and the setup resembled a small beauty supply store, a great selling point for when I planned day excursions here. I took advantage of the display of products, including sunscreen and body spray. Chloe would love this.

As soon as I exited the restroom, I heard two people arguing around the corner. I didn't mean to eavesdrop, but it was hard not to. I paused before heading back to Chloe.

"You're such a liar," a woman said.

Wait, was that Kelsey's voice?

"Why are you even here?" a man's voice slurred.

That's Phillip.

"Why does it bother you so much? Are you afraid I might have a talk with your precious Josie? Worried she might find out the truth about who you really are?"

"Do what you have to do," Phillip said sharply. "You really think Josie cares what you have to say? I have news for you—no one cares. The only reason you were invited was so I wouldn't have to hear it from my parents."

I carefully peeked around the corner, and sure enough, the voices belonged to Phillip and Kelsey.

Kelsey inched closer to Phillip and shoved her finger in his face. "Go to hell, Phillip. I can't wait for karma to finally catch up to you. You'll get everything you deserve. I promise you."

She started to walk away from him, and I quickly ran to join Chloe before someone saw me.

"Several of my friends have stayed here, and they've raved about it," Chloe said. She was still monopolizing the bartender's time. As amazing as this resort was, we needed to head back to the ship soon. I was still working, and with Jack hanging around, I had to stay on top of my responsibilities.

I was still trying to catch my breath as I flopped down in my seat.

Chloe gave me a funny look. "What's the matter?"

I shook my head as I inhaled slowly. "Nothing."

"Then why were you running and from whom?"

I looked around to see if I could spot Phillip or Kelsey, but thankfully the coast was clear.

"Tell you later." I paused and took a sip of my drink. "What are you two talking about?"

Chloe got my hint and introduced me to her new friend, Bjorn the bartender.

I pretended to listen to their conversation about the Paradise Island Resort and other destinations in the Caribbean, but I was distracted as I looked around. I didn't see Phillip, Kelsey, or Josie. That made me wonder if Kelsey had followed through on her threat and gone to talk to Josie.

Maybe Chloe was right and there was more behind Kelsey and her relationship with the newlyweds. It didn't matter because their drama was none of my business. My responsibility was to ensure our guests were content and having a good time while on vacation—that included Josie, Phillip, Bobby, and Michelle.

I scanned the pool area and saw Michelle, who was posing and taking selfies with two other girls I'd briefly met. At least she looked like she was enjoying herself.

"Lexi, can you explain to this gentleman why our cruise line is superior? He claims he's heard different."

I gave the bartender a surprised look. "Really? What exactly did you hear?"

This was the type of information Jack would want to know, the things our previous guests have said about us versus about our competition. I could go back to him and relay all this information and research. That would show him exactly how good I am at my job and why he should leave me in my position.

The bartender shook his head. "Take it easy. I heard from a couple who stayed here that the other cruise lines care more about their guests. They said Epic Cruise Line is more expensive but doesn't offer anything more than the other companies."

"Well, I can assure you that's not true," I insisted. "I'm here to make sure our guests are receiving the best possible service. I haven't heard of other cruise lines sending their staff members to make sure guests are being taken care of."

Bjorn the bartender didn't need to know that Josie had asked me to stop by or that we'd sat next to each other in Mr. Stanley's fourth-grade class.

"And the entertainment on Epic is by far the best in the industry," Chloe declared. She wasn't just being overconfident. Our performers were top-notch, and our entertainment staff had been featured frequently by top travel bloggers.

"Absolutely," I agreed. "Our musicians are the best out there."

Chloe playfully bowed.

Bjorn cracked a smile. "Don't get me wrong... I've talked to plenty of people who say they would only sail with your company."

"Aha!" Chloe shouted.

The bartender laughed. *Seriously?* Was he just trying to get a reaction out of us? If so, it totally worked. Our conversation continued as both Chloe and I raved about everything our cruise line had to offer. I wished Jack were here to see us in action.

Out of the corner of my eye, I noticed Josie pacing in the far corner of the pool deck. She was staring at her phone with a concerned look on her face. She was no longer with her friends, and for some reason I felt like I should make sure she was okay. I told Chloe I'd be back, although I didn't think she heard a word I said. She was now in a serious, but friendly, debate with Bjorn about why cruising was the best kind of vacation. Thankfully she was still nursing her first cocktail—the last thing I needed was for her to drink too much in front of our guests.

"Hey, Josie."

She turned toward me. "Hi, Lexi. Oh no. Are you leaving already? I'm sorry we didn't get to spend more time together."

I waved my hand. "Don't worry about it. Are *you* okay?"

She bowed her head. "I'm fine. Just dealing with some family stuff back home. I really shouldn't be worrying about it while I'm here..."

I gave her a sympathetic nod, but she kept talking.

"Phillip keeps telling me to ignore it, and I'm really trying, but it's difficult when—" She paused and looked around.

I assumed she didn't want anyone else to hear what she was about to say.

She motioned for me to walk with her. "Sorry. There are a lot of close family friends here, and the last thing I need is for the wrong person to overhear me complain about Phillip's family. He's already frustrated today."

His argument with Kelsey popped into my mind, but I didn't bring it up.

"Let me guess. Phillip's mother is difficult?" I asked. "I've heard the mother-in-law relationship can be complicated. Isn't there a saying—you don't just marry the man, you marry his family, too. Maybe you need to give it some time."

Josie sighed. "It's not just his mother. It's all of them. His father, aunts and uncles, grandparents. His brother—you met Drew—is the only one who's been nice to me. The family is very wealthy, and of course they think I only married Phillip for his money. Which isn't true, I swear. Phillip says he's talked to them about it, but they haven't let up."

I frowned. "I'm sorry. I'm sure it isn't easy to be accused of such a thing."

"I even went to talk to his parents a few nights before the wedding, but I think it made everything worse. Phillip has been patient, but I know it's wearing on him because they're a very tight-knit family." She paused. "What am I doing? You don't want to hear about this stuff. It's difficult because Phillip and I agreed not to say anything to our friends about it. He wants to maintain a good image for our community, our business, and his family."

I patted her arm. "It's okay. Sometimes it's easier to talk to people we don't know as well."

And I didn't know Josie now. The last time I saw her we were little girls. I felt bad for her, though. Here she was, supposed to be celebrating her new life, but instead she was worrying about maintaining the perfect image in front of the people closest to her.

"Anyway, I hate to say it, but I don't know if it's ever going to get better," she said sadly. "I've never done anything to make them hate me as much as they do, and I don't know how to fix it."

I listened to Josie as we turned the corner, when something—actually, someone—in the hot tub caught my eye.

Wait, is that...?

Through the bubbles I saw a figure floating facedown. The only movement I noticed was the rushing of the water. I felt my body break into a cold sweat as I knew what was happening in front of my eyes.

"Oh, no!" I exclaimed.

"Lexi?" Josie asked worriedly.

Suddenly a surge of adrenaline pulsed through my body as I raced toward the hot tub. Without a second thought, I jumped into the hot, bubbling water in my clothes. The jolt of the extreme temperature took over as I lifted the person's head out of the water, giving me the first glimpse of the drowning victim's face. I gasped when I realized it was Phillip. His eyes were closed, and he wasn't moving. I used every ounce of my strength to push the motionless body out of the water. Almost breathless, I started to pull myself out of the hot tub when poor Josie fell down to her knees beside her husband.

"What's happening?" she screamed as she shook him. "Phillip? Phillip, answer me."

"Josie, try to stay calm," I begged.

Easier said than done. Her husband wasn't moving or responding to her voice.

"We need some help over here!" I screamed. "Please, help. Someone call 9-1-1!"

I quickly began alternating between breathing into his mouth and checking for a pulse. Over and over again I repeated this cycle, but he wasn't responding.

"Phillip, open your eyes!" Josie screamed through her tears. Someone came and pulled her away, but I didn't look up to see who it was.

"What's going on?" a man's voice asked. "Did he drown?"

I ignored the questions that were becoming more desperate as I heard people shouting and crying. I didn't look up but continued my attempts to resuscitate Phillip. The urgency to save him was the only thing on my mind while his poor wife and friends watched me. As I continued working on him, doubt crept into my mind. I silently prayed he'd open his eyes, but it wasn't happening. What if this man died right here in front of his loved ones? They needed me to come through for them. I had to.

"Does she know what she's doing?" someone screamed.

"We need a doctor," another guest shouted.

"She's a lifeguard," Chloe yelled. "He's in good hands."

"Save him, Lexi. Please save him," Josie wailed.

Over and over again, I repeated the steps I'd been trained to do, desperately trying to make this man breathe again, and I didn't stop until the paramedics arrived.

I sat back on the pool deck and watched as they continued the rescue efforts on Phillip's still body. The water dripped from my soaked hair and clothing, and the taste of chlorine was still on my lips. I was exhausted and horrified that I wasn't able to revive him. When I finally looked up, I saw Josie with tears streaming down her cheeks, standing with Phillip's brother, who was trying to calm her down.

"Lexi, are you okay?" Chloe asked, her hand on my shoulder.

I shook my head. I just wanted to wake up from this horrific moment and be back on the ship.

Phillip Edwards was dead, and as hard as I'd tried, I couldn't save him.

CHAPTER THREE

———

I pulled the towel tightly around me as I listened to the same questions over and over again. My head was pounding, my wet clothes clung uncomfortably to my body, and I felt like I was on trial. I understood the authorities needed to ask me questions, but I'd much rather have answered them while wearing some comfortable, dry clothes.

"I was talking to Phillip's wife, and we were walking by the hot tub. That's when I noticed something under the bubbles," I said. "I didn't realize it was him until after I jumped in and pushed him out of the water."

"Did you see anyone else near the hot tub? Or maybe leaving the area?"

I shrugged. The only thing I could remember was Josie talking about Phillip's family. I'd been so focused on what she was saying, I hadn't looked to see if anyone was there.

"I don't remember. We were having a conversation, so I wasn't really paying attention to anything else."

"You said you're a certified lifeguard with Epic Cruise Line?" the officer asked. "But you were invited by Josie Edwards to come here today?"

I nodded. "Well, yes, but I was actually coming to the island anyway to follow up with our contact here at the resort. I met with Phillip and Josie last night and made all the arrangements for their activities while we were here. Our cruise line has an agreement with this resort that allows our guests to book day trips here and use the facilities."

"And you just met Mrs. Edwards for the first time last night?"

"Not exactly. We actually know each other from childhood, but I haven't seen her in years." I paused. "After I made their arrangements, Josie invited me to stop by since I was going to be off the ship. They were already meeting up with friends who are staying here. It was supposed to be a little post-wedding celebration."

The officer continued to make notes as I repeated all the details of our conversation from the night before.

I was physically and emotionally exhausted. I knew I needed to hold it together, but I was struggling. I was an employee of Epic Cruise Line, and one of our passengers had just died. I kept replaying those chaotic moments in my head. Should I have done something else? Had I done everything I could to save him? The worst part was I kept hearing Josie's voice pleading with me to save her husband. I'd failed her, and I'd failed the company. Even though we weren't on the ship, it was my responsibility to protect our passengers. Their safety was supposed to be our number one priority.

"Here you go," Chloe said as she handed me a bottle of water.

Chloe had been very supportive. I don't know what I would've done if she hadn't come with me. While I'd been answering questions, she'd been contacting the ship to let them know what happened.

"Have you seen Josie?" I asked her.

She shook her head. "Not since they took her and Phillip's brother inside."

I frowned. "I can't believe this is happening."

She patted me on the shoulder. "I know you probably don't want to hear this right now, but you were amazing. You didn't give up on him. Everyone who was at the pool could see that."

I shrugged. "But it wasn't enough."

She moved closer to me. "So, I was doing a bit of eavesdropping, and it sounded like they aren't exactly sure what happened to Phillip," she whispered. "Whether he fell in or passed out. And remember these people have been drinking all day. I wouldn't be shocked if he was so smashed that he got into the hot tub and fell asleep."

I knew she was right. I didn't doubt Phillip had had plenty to drink throughout the day, but there was something else that'd been bothering me. Why was Phillip all by himself in a hot tub, especially at an event where he was surrounded by friends and his wife? I kept going back to the conversation I'd overheard between him and Kelsey. And where was Kelsey? I hadn't seen her since she'd argued with Phillip.

"I think it's odd that he would be hanging out by himself in a hot tub," I said out loud.

Chloe gave me a curious look. "What are you saying?"

I shrugged. "I don't know what I'm saying. This is so awful. A day that should have been a celebration for Josie and Phillip has ended in tragedy. I'm so heartbroken for her. I keep hearing her voice over and over again in my head. I couldn't even look up at her when I was giving him CPR."

Chloe frowned. "I can't imagine what that kind of pressure feels like."

I closed my eyes. "There's nothing like it."

Since being on the *Legend* for two years, I'd jumped into the pools to use my lifeguard skills a handful of times. Most of the time children slipped under the water or ended up getting turned around on the slides. But Epic Cruise Line was extremely diligent with their training. Our lifeguard staff was constantly doing life-saving drills and keeping up with our skill tests. I'd felt completely prepared to jump into action, but again it may have been too late by the time I came upon the scene.

"Well, hopefully we can leave soon," Chloe said. "I'm sure you're ready. They're sending someone from the ship to talk to the authorities."

I groaned. "Did they say who was coming?"

She shook her head. "No, but I'm sure they want to do damage control."

I wasn't so naive to think there wouldn't be news about Phillip's death. This was a situation the media would have a field day with.

"I think we're finished with our questions for the moment," the officer said, rejoining Chloe and me. "But please don't leave yet. We may need more information as we continue speaking with the guests."

I tried not to show my disappointment. Obviously I wasn't heading back to the ship anytime soon. I was miserable in my wet clothes, though. Maybe I could ask the resort for a robe or something in the meantime.

"Let's get some food while we wait," Chloe suggested.

"I'm not hungry."

She ignored me as she dragged me over to where a few of the Edwards' friends were still hanging around. As expected, the mood had completely shifted, and everyone was talking quietly among themselves. I saw Michelle and another one of Josie's bride tribe sitting with their heads together. I still didn't see Kelsey. Maybe she was with Josie and Drew.

"You need to eat something, and I'll find out if I can get you some dry clothes."

"Yes, please," I said gratefully. "Thanks for being here, Chloe."

She reached over and squeezed my arm. "There's no chance I'd let you go through this alone."

After Chloe went off in search of food and dry clothing for me, I was about to sit down at a table when I noticed Phillip's friend Bobby scrolling through his phone. He had a drink in his hand but looked like he could barely stand up straight.

Once again I felt the guilt stab through me. Bobby was another person I'd let down. Josie said they'd been best friends since before they could walk. I couldn't begin to imagine how devastated he must've been feeling. I wanted to tell him how sorry I was that I couldn't do more for his friend. Our guests depended on me to step up and save them, and in Phillip's case, I hadn't followed through.

I hesitated before I finally decided to approach him. "Excuse me."

Bobby looked up from his phone. "Lifeguard girl," he exclaimed as he swayed back and forth.

I definitely didn't care for his greeting, especially given the situation. But I could tell by the way he could barely stand that he'd had his share of drinks today as well.

"I don't want to bother you, but I wanted to tell you how sorry I am about Phillip."

"It is what it is," he said as he avoided eye contact with me.

I didn't want to make things worse, so I was about to walk away when he continued talking.

"You want to know what the worst part of this is?" he growled.

I pressed my lips together. I had a feeling he was about to tell me.

"Phil had to control everything. He had to be the best, the top dog no matter what the cost, and look where it got him. Everything he wanted isn't important anymore, and I hope it was worth it."

Okay, so I had no idea what this guy was talking about, but he'd sparked my curiosity.

"Can I ask you something, lifeguard girl?"

Ugh. I really wished he'd stop calling me that.

"Sure," I said through gritted teeth.

"Do you ever wonder why things like this happen to people?"

I gave him a sympathetic look. "Of course. Tragedies always make me question why bad things happen to good people."

He snorted as he swayed to the side, and I began to wonder if he was going to fall over.

"Yeah, right. *Good* people. Well, you didn't know Phil like I did," he said with a chuckle.

I chewed on my bottom lip. "No, I didn't. But he seemed to care. I mean, he wanted to share this special time in his life with all of you. You were important to him."

Bobby shook his head. "Nope. He wanted to show off, like always. His success was more important than anything else. Definitely more important than his friendships."

Hold on a minute. Weren't Bobby and Phillip supposed to be besties forever?

"He didn't listen when we told him not to marry Josie. Everyone told him it was a mistake." He added, "I warned him, but nope, he never cared about what I had to say. And supposedly I was his best friend."

What was he saying? So Bobby didn't support their marriage either? Was I missing something?

"Why was it a mistake for him to marry Josie?" I asked nonchalantly. "I haven't seen Josie since we were young, but she and Phillip seem very much in love."

"Lexi."

I turned around to see Chloe motioning for me to join her. *Crap.* Bobby was certainly in the mood to talk, and I wanted to hear more about Josie. *Why did everyone have an issue with her?* And how could Phillip have invited Bobby to go on the cruise with them, knowing how he felt about his wife? I wondered if Josie knew how Bobby really felt about her. They'd all seemed to be really close when she'd introduced them to us. Was it all just a big act?

"Lexi. Jack's here," she called eagerly.

Jack? Oh great, that's all I needed right now. I should've known he'd be the person to come from the *Legend*. This situation was absolutely in his area of expertise.

"I'm sorry to cut you off," I told Bobby. "Please let us know if we can do anything for you once you return to the ship. I can assure you that the cruise line will do everything we can to accommodate you, Michelle, and Josie."

He looked at his phone and hobbled away without another word.

As I walked toward Chloe, I tried to make some sense out of the conversation I'd just had with Bobby. Even though he was drunk, he was obviously angry with his friend. Their issues seemed to run deeper than a simple disagreement. By the way he was talking, it almost seemed like he thought Phillip deserved this fate. I was especially confused about the comments he'd made regarding Josie and their marriage. Not to mention, Kelsey certainly acted like she didn't care for Josie either. And what about that disagreement I overheard between Kelsey and Phillip? It was all too much to wrap my brain around. Although I hadn't seen Josie since we were nine years old, she seemed like the same fun-loving girl I remembered. Bobby, Kelsey, and Phillip's family—they obviously saw something different. Was there another side to her I didn't know? Just because she was my best friend all those years ago didn't make her a saint. I had no idea of the type of person she'd grown up to be.

"What was that about?" Chloe asked as she pointed to where I had just been talking to Bobby.

I turned around to look at him, but he was already gone. "I'm trying to figure that out myself. I wanted to give him my condolences, but the guy is completely wasted. He was in the middle of rambling on about Phillip and Josie when you called me over. Apparently he doesn't like Josie and tried to convince Phillip not to marry her."

Chloe gave me a confused look. "Why?"

I shook my head. "I'm not sure. It was a strange conversation. He told me he'd tried to warn Phillip, but he wouldn't listen. I was about to find out more when you called me over."

"I'm sorry. I figured you'd want to know Jack was here. I saw him talking to the police."

I sighed. "Of course Jack is here. He and I just had a conversation about how my visit could be good exposure for the cruise line. Building relationships so our guests would return to sail with us. Obviously that's not the case for Phillip Edwards. And let's be honest, I doubt Josie will return again. She just lost her husband. What kind of traumatic memories is she going to have from this trip?"

Chloe put her arm around my shoulders. "Lexi, none of this is your fault."

I placed my hands on my forehead. "Chloe, did you not see what happened? I couldn't save him," I exclaimed. "I know his death isn't my fault, but this could've easily happened on the ship. What about the faith and trust our company has put in me for the last two years? Do you really think they're going to put me out on the lifeguard stand tomorrow?"

She sighed. "Well, maybe not tomorrow. I'm sure they'll give you a break. You've been through a harrowing ordeal, which was completely out of your control. And remember, it may have been too late for *anyone* to save him."

I knew she was right, but it was still difficult not to think about what I could've done differently. I took a few deep breaths as I mentally prepared myself to talk to Jack. I didn't know why the thought of that made me so nervous. Maybe it was because I'd been so confident I would do a good job looking after our guests today. In the back of my mind I recalled our conversation and how he'd said he put together the departments on other ships. Jack mentioned he planned on organizing new teams on our ship. I wondered if my position with the Port Adventures team was in jeopardy, and to add to my stress, now I was worried about my lifeguard job.

"I know you're right, but now I have to face Jack."

She raised her eyebrows. "And that's a bad thing? I mean, he is rather attractive."

I rubbed my temples with my fingertips, conveniently ignoring Chloe's comment about Jack being attractive. "Yes, it's a bad thing because it's his job to protect the reputation of our cruise line. I'm sure the media would love to know about the death of one of our passengers."

Out of the corner of my eye I noticed Jack was coming toward us. I took a deep breath and turned to meet up with him. "Hello, Jack," I said in my most professional voice.

"Hi. Are you both alright?" he asked. He sounded concerned, but I wasn't sure if he was concerned about Chloe and me or about the company. Probably a little of both. He was wearing a gray pinstriped dress shirt with a gray tie, and of course he looked completely out of place at a resort pool.

Chloe said yes, and I agreed.

"The police explained what happened, but I wanted to hear it directly from you. It sounds like you've had quite an eventful day."

Eventful was one way to describe it.

I took a deep breath and then launched into the same story I'd told the officer.

"Josie and I were talking when we found Phillip in the hot tub. I didn't know it was him at first, and then everything happened so fast."

Jack listened intently as I relived those gut-wrenching moments once again. With each detail I gave him, my voice shook and my heart pounded.

"I tried to revive him," I wailed. "I followed my training step by step. I'm thinking it was probably already too late by the time we got to him, but it didn't matter." I tried to swallow the lump that had risen in my throat. "If only we had found him a few minutes sooner—"

"She really did everything she could," Chloe interrupted. "You should have seen her. She kept working on him until the paramedics arrived. She never gave up."

I gave her a grateful smile. "I didn't know how long he had been under," I added. "I just reacted as soon as I saw him in the water. It's a natural inclination for me to jump into action when I see someone underwater."

Jack listened intently. I wondered if that was the same thing the police had told him.

"Have the police said if they know what happened to Phillip?" I asked. I began to feel nervous, like I was suddenly being watched very carefully.

"Not yet, but it sounds like they might be launching a full investigation," Jack stated. "According to the officer, his family has been notified and are asking that everyone who was present be questioned extensively. They want to know how this happened, which is understandable. Such a terrible tragedy."

I bit my lower lip. "I'm not surprised, based on what I've heard about them."

Chloe gave me a funny look. "What do you know about his family?"

I looked back and forth between Chloe and Jack. "Well, not much other than what Josie said. She told me they are wealthy and they didn't think she was good enough to marry their son. Their friend Bobby alluded to the same thing. There was also something strange going on between Phillip and his friend Kelsey."

Jack shook his head. "Their personal lives are not my concern right now. What is concerning is that you, as a representative of Epic Cruise Line, are now a part of this investigation. We have to consider possible liability issues of your involvement and the affect it could have on the cruise line. You were working during your visit to the resort today. You also said you were with his wife when he was discovered in the hot tub, isn't that right?"

That was exactly what I was afraid of. Whether I liked it or not, I was involved.

"Yes, I was. She looked upset, so I was checking on her before heading back to the ship. After all, that's the reason I'm here." I stopped talking as Jack pulled his phone out of his pocket. He frowned, which worried me. "I told you I did everything I could to save him. All of the witnesses can attest to that."

"I'm sure you did," Jack replied. "The authorities mentioned your connection with Mr. Edwards' wife. I'm concerned it might come into question should a full investigation arise."

I felt a sudden tightness in my chest. Could my past connection to Josie become a factor in the investigation of his sudden death? Why? A wave of nausea had suddenly taken hold of my stomach, making me want to throw up.

I looked at Chloe. She had a concerned expression on her face. I felt so terrible that I'd dragged her into this. She'd agreed to come, but ultimately it was my fault she was here.

I folded my arms. "You knew I was coming here today. We discussed this being an important part of my job. You even agreed it would be good for me to stop by and make sure the Edwards were satisfied with their experience and to ensure they'd return to cruise with us again. Don't you remember our conversation?"

"Of course I do."

"Then why are you acting like I committed a crime?" I snapped.

Chloe rubbed my back. "As you can imagine, Lexi's been through quite a shock."

Jack's face softened. "I'm not dismissing your heroic efforts, nor am I dismissing the difficulty of your experience. But it's my responsibility to ensure the cruise line and all employees are protected."

Hmm…I wasn't feeling protected at that moment. I tightened my jaw as I tried to make sense of what he was telling me. It sounded like my connection to Josie could be the potential issue here. Which could only mean one thing: Was Phillip's family looking for someone to blame for his death, and was that someone his wife?

CHAPTER FOUR

———

It felt like the day was never going to end. The police, the news crews, the tears, and the whisperings. It was so overwhelming. I was ready to leave this resort, and I never wanted to come back. Although I knew there wasn't a chance of that happening just yet.

Once the sailing was over, we'd start all over again with another new group of passengers. I'd be booking new excursions at this resort, assuming Jack didn't fill my position with someone else. I was already thinking about what I would say if guests asked me about what happened at the Paradise Island Resort. Honesty was always the best policy, and I had nothing to hide.

I sat in silence on a pool lounger as I waited for the police to continue questioning the other witnesses. Chloe had found me a robe from the hotel concierge, but it had taken so long that my sundress was already mostly dried. My hair was frizzy and matted down against my head, and when I finally went to the bathroom I nearly cried when I saw my reflection in the mirror. My mascara was smudged under my right eye, and I looked exactly like I felt. Awful.

I cleaned myself up the best way I could and tried to look as presentable as possible. It wasn't going to help the credibility of Epic Cruise Line if I looked like a train wreck.

Jack had been busy doing damage control, as the media had already gotten the news of Phillip's drowning. The authorities were doing a good job keeping things calm, but the questions were flying. I hated watching it from the sidelines, because I was the one who'd found Phillip. I wanted to step in and help, but I held back because it was Jack's responsibility to field those questions. The police had taped off the area around the hot tub, and I saw them walking around and taking photos.

I still hadn't seen Josie, but Chloe found out she was with friends and was okay. I wanted to talk to her and tell her how sorry I was. In my mind I went over several different scenarios and what ifs. I kept coming back to the fact that Phillip was alone in the hot tub, and what if we had gotten to him sooner? I wondered if things would've been different if I'd checked on Josie earlier instead of having the best cruise line debate with Chloe and Bjorn the bartender. I couldn't help but think about how upset Josie had been when I saw her right before we found Phillip. She never told me if they'd had an argument or what had sparked her telling me about her issues with his family. And what about all the warnings that Phillip had received about marrying Josie? Would this whole situation somehow fall on her shoulders, especially now when she was about to bury her new husband? The questions were endless. I was going to drive myself crazy if I didn't stop.

Chloe quietly sat next to me, looking at her phone.

"Why don't you find out if you can you go back to the ship? You've already given your statement."

She shook her head. "I'm not leaving you."

I gave her a grateful smile. "I'm fine. I promise. I'll probably be here for a while anyway, or I'll at least have to stay as long as Jack does. If they give you the green light to leave, you should go for it." I knew she wanted to get out of there as badly as I did.

After a bit of hesitating, she gave me a hug and went to talk to the detective.

I closed my eyes and exhaled. Sitting around and not doing anything productive was awful. I wanted to check on Josie. Even though Jack had mentioned my connection with her could come into question, I didn't care. Avoiding her wasn't going to change what happened.

When I walked past Jack, I motioned to him that I would be right back, and he gave me a half nod. I felt kind of weird leaving the pool area, but I shouldn't have because I wasn't a prisoner. They'd asked me to stick around the resort, and that's what I was doing.

When I entered the hotel, I climbed the elegant wrought iron staircase toward the lobby. It really was a stunning property. Wall-to-wall pristine white marble flooring, lots of windows, and large glass doors that opened to the beach. There were lush white couches and sparkling chandeliers sprinkled throughout. Everything was bright, open, and cheerful—yet somehow I felt a dark cloud hung over it with Phillip's death. I'd been here many times before, but today it seemed different. I'd probably never forget this place. I wondered if I'd feel the sadness every time I came here. Would guests not want to visit because of the Epic Cruise Line guest who drowned? Would the memories of Phillip's death haunt me for years to come?

I was about to ask the concierge where I could find Josie, when I saw Michelle and another girl from the bride tribe. Of course, I couldn't remember her name. I should've paid better attention when Josie was doing the introductions.

Both Michelle and her friend looked like they were contestants on *The Bachelor*. Their makeup was perfectly applied, and not one hair on their heads was out of place. Maybe they were trying to look good in case any reporters asked them questions? Then again, they hadn't jumped into a hot tub with their clothes on or tried to save a man's life.

"Michelle, hi."

She gave me a nonchalant wave as I walked toward her. I wasn't sure if she even remembered me.

"I was looking for Josie. Have you seen her?"

"She's in the St. Thomas Meeting Room," she replied, lowering her voice. A serious expression spread across her face. "She's trying to stay clear of the media, poor thing. She knows people want to help, but it's all very overwhelming right now. It's wild to think that the future she *thought* she was going to have with Phillip is gone. She had so many plans, and now..." She paused and shook her head.

Hmm...I'd always thought I was a good judge of people, but I couldn't read Michelle.

She was saying all the right things, but I didn't get the feeling she cared as much as she was acting like she did. Everyone handled grief differently, but her behavior seemed a bit staged. She looked extremely put together for someone who just lost a very close friend. I knew she was supposed to be Bobby's girlfriend, but I hadn't seen them interact much. And she didn't seem the least bit fazed when he'd been flirting with Chloe. Was she good friends with Josie, or was that friendship because of Phillip and Bobby? Based on what other people thought of Josie, I wondered if Michelle was pretending to be her friend too.

"I can't imagine how Josie's feeling," I said. "Were you close to Phillip?"

"Yes," she exclaimed. "Absolutely. We were all very close. Basically family."

She started to fan her face, and all of sudden she looked like she might start crying.

It suddenly occurred to me that Michelle was also one of our guests on the ship. It was my job to look after her as well. "How about you? Is there anything I can do for you and Bobby? I'm sure this has been very difficult for him."

Michelle frowned, and there were no tears to be shed. "Your guess is as good as mine. He's probably sleeping it off somewhere."

Hmm…it wouldn't have surprised me. He could barely stand when I'd spoken to him earlier. But her reaction was still strange. She didn't show an ounce of compassion for her boyfriend, considering his friend had just drowned.

"Oh, I figured he might need moral support right now"—I paused—"since he was Phillip's best friend."

Michelle looked at the other girl, who hadn't said anything yet.

"Who knows? Phillip and Bobby had a love-hate relationship. And Bobby can be a real jerk sometimes…" the girl added.

This didn't come as a shock to me. Bobby hadn't spoken fondly of Phillip during his drunken ramble.

"I haven't checked on him yet," Michelle said. "We got into an argument this morning. It was really stupid, but until he's ready to apologize for the things he said and not act like a stupid drunk, I have nothing to say to him."

Seriously? An unspeakable tragedy had occurred. Why wouldn't Michelle check on her boyfriend? It didn't seem like the appropriate time to hold a grudge or be mad at him. Although he was blatantly flirting with Chloe in front of her when we met them, so what did I know? And another argument? Between Phillip, Kelsey, and Bobby—there certainly seemed to be a lot of holes in this tight-knit group.

"Anyway, thank you for checking on us," Michelle said before slipping away with her friend.

I stood still while trying to make sense of our odd interaction. This was an emotional situation for all parties involved, so I had no right to judge the way anyone handled it.

I followed the signs for the St. Thomas Meeting Room. I wanted to talk to Josie, but I didn't want to be gone too long. I especially didn't want to add more questions about my friendship with Josie, just in case.

When I entered the small room, I noticed a few chairs and a couch set up along the wall. There was a food cart, and a few hotel employees were milling around. Josie was sitting on the couch with Phillip's brother. I recalled her telling me he was the only member of Phillip's family who was nice to her.

Drew was saying something to her, and she was nodding her head. She had changed out of her tiny bathing suit and was wearing a light blue maxi dress. Her hair was pulled back into a ponytail, and it didn't look like she had any makeup on. She looked very calm though, almost peaceful, which struck me as a little odd. Truthfully, I didn't know what I was expecting her to look like. I guess I'd envisioned her being inconsolable, with mascara tears streaming down her face.

I paused in the doorway as my heart began to race. Would she get upset seeing me there? What if she blamed me for not saving her husband? And what about Drew? I hadn't even considered what he was feeling—his brother had just died. I imagined he was also having to deal with the rest of his family who weren't there, and based on what I'd heard so far, it didn't sound easy.

With a deep breath, I walked toward them. As soon as Josie saw me, she stood up, rushed toward me, and gave me a hug.

"Lexi, I was wondering if you were still here," she said into my neck. "Come sit down. Do you want some coffee or something else to drink? I can probably get you anything you want. The staff is being so kind."

I followed her to the couch where Drew was waiting. "I'm fine right now, but thank you," I replied. I sat in one of the chairs. I felt very anxious, but before I had a chance to say anything, Drew began talking.

"I'm sorry we haven't had a chance to speak to you," he said. "It's been utter chaos since—"

I held up my hand. "Oh, I know. Please don't apologize."

He didn't owe me an explanation. They were the ones who were now grieving.

"Lexi, we want to thank you for trying to save my brother," Drew said as he got choked up. He looked away and cleared his throat.

"That's why I wanted to talk to you," I replied. "I needed to tell you how sorry I am that I couldn't do more for Phillip. I promise I did everything I was trained to do. I just wish it had turned out differently…"

"We know you did," Josie said sympathetically.

"Of course," Drew added. "This is a terrible situation that no one was prepared for. And I was very impressed with your efforts. Your company is lucky to have you."

They were being so nice, I wanted to cry. But I needed to hold my tears in for a little while longer. "How is your family doing?" I asked Drew.

He sighed and glanced at Josie. "Not good. My parents are devastated, of course. They're pushing hard for a full investigation to be conducted. I tried to explain that Phil had had a lot to drink and he most likely passed out, but they don't want to hear it. They're angry, so they want to blame someone."

"I'm sure they blame me," Josie interjected. "They didn't want Phillip and me to get married in the first place, and we came to the Bahamas to celebrate our marriage."

I raised my eyebrows. I knew they didn't like her, but would they actually blame Josie for his death?

"Did they say they think it's your fault?" I asked. I glanced at Drew. His face had grown pale. He didn't answer my question, but he didn't deny it either.

"I love my husband, whether they believe it or not," Josie interjected as she clenched her fists. Tears filled her eyes as she covered her face.

"They're just very emotional right now," Drew said unconvincingly.

I could tell by Drew's face that he didn't believe what he was saying.

"What exactly do they think happened to him?" I asked. "I mean, he was in the hot tub. He could have slipped and fallen in or, like you said, passed out."

"Exactly," Josie wailed.

Drew's phone rang. He looked at the screen and stood up. "It's my father's attorney. I better take this."

Josie waved him away. When she picked up her coffee cup, I noticed her hands were shaking. Maybe caffeine wasn't the best thing for her just now. However, other than her hands, she seemed relatively calm.

"Josie, can I get you something else?"

She shook her head. "No, thank you though."

We both grew quiet as I tried to come up with the right words. There was nothing I could say to fix it or make it better. I was reminded of the conversation we'd been having when we found Phillip. Josie was here surrounded by Phillip's family and friends. I wondered if she was getting any support. I knew she had her bride tribe, but that included Bobby's girlfriend. I still wasn't sure who were her friends and who was there because of Phillip or his family. Kelsey definitely wasn't there for her.

"Have you contacted your family yet?" I asked. "Or is there someone I can call for you?"

She tilted her head down. "I spoke to my mother. She wanted to come down here, but I told her not to."

I gave her a curious look. "Why? Don't you think it'd be helpful to have your family with you for support?"

With her shaking hand, she placed the coffee cup down on the side table. "I don't want to drag her into this. She's had a lot of health problems and doesn't need any more stress. The wedding was hard enough on her."

"Your wedding?"

She pursed her lips. "Yes. Madeline and Andrew, those are Phillip's parents, made things very difficult for us. At one point my mother asked me if I was sure I wanted to go through with it. She was so angry and frustrated with the whole situation, but I begged her not to say anything. I didn't want to add any fuel to the fire, and his parents were looking for anything to stir the pot. I wanted to get married and start my life with Phillip."

Wow. Were these people really so horrible for her mother to question their marriage? It seemed like the odds were stacked against her no matter what.

"Anyway, my mother's been through a lot and undergone extensive medical treatment. Coming here just to sit with me wouldn't do any good. I don't want my mom to be anywhere near this if it gets ugly."

My heart really went out to her. "Josie, I can't begin to pretend I understand what you're going through. And I'm sorry about your mom."

"Thanks." She dropped her head. "Anyway, I keep thinking about how painful this must be for everyone else. I'm sure Bobby is heartbroken."

I thought about the conversation I'd had with Bobby earlier. He hadn't seemed heartbroken at all, but I'd never have told Josie that.

"Oh, of course. Have you talked to him?"

"Not yet, but like I told you, they've been close their whole lives. Anyway, I'm glad Bobby and Drew are here. It makes me feel closer to Phillip, and I can use all the friends I can get right now."

Except they weren't her friends. Bobby was upset with him about something and had even tried to warn Phillip not to marry her. And I'd overheard Phillip and Kelsey arguing. It was clear Josie didn't know how his "friends" really felt about her. And Drew was Phillip's brother. Wouldn't he be loyal to his family?

"Thank you for being here today, Lexi. You have no idea how comforting it is. I feel like it was meant to be for us to see other again after all these years."

I wished I felt the same way. As cool as it was to see Josie again, I wished I weren't part of this tragedy. The more I learned, the more complicated this situation seemed. Not only was I facing potential issues with my jobs, but I suddenly felt like I'd been thrust into the very complicated personal situation of this woman I barely knew. I didn't want to add to her stress, but I felt I should tell her what Jack had said.

"There's something else you should know," I told her.

She gave me a worried look. "Okay, what?"

I cleared my throat. "The cruise line's director of public relations is concerned that our connection might come into question if there's a formal investigation. I guess because you invited me here and then I was with you when we found Phillip in the hot tub. He's worried about possible liability issues, being that I was working at the time I tried to revive Phillip."

She sighed and leaned her head against the couch. "I heard something about that, and I don't know what to say. It's not fair because you were just being a good human and doing your job."

Yes, I was. After all the training I'd had, it was a natural response to jump in and save a drowning victim. I had no idea I could be stepping into a family war. It didn't matter though, because I wouldn't have done anything differently in that moment. I'd made a commitment to save lives, and I'd do it again in a heartbeat.

"Josie, I know you told me that Phillip's parents didn't support your marriage, but do you really believe they'd blame you?"

Josie's face twisted. "Their sons are their pride and joy. They never thought I was good enough for their baby—they believed I was only with him for his money. Nothing could be further from the truth, Lexi. Phillip went against their wishes, and here we are. Maybe he should've listened. This never would've happened if we hadn't gotten married."

"My apologies for leaving so abruptly," Drew said, interrupting our conversation. He flopped down on the couch and pinched the bridge of his nose. He looked completely exhausted.

"What did the lawyer say?" Josie asked. She didn't appear as calm as she'd been a few minutes before, but at least she wasn't holding hot coffee anymore.

"They're putting a rush on the medical exam results. They're hoping some closure will at least bring peace of mind."

Josie's face twisted, and she didn't seem as calm as she did when I'd first arrived. I was beginning to wonder what, if anything, those medical results were going to reveal. And there was a tiny part of me that wondered if there was some validity to their concerns. Was there more to Phillip's drowning than an unfortunate accident, and if so, who would want him dead?

CHAPTER FIVE

It had been fewer than twenty-four hours since I'd booked Phillip and Josie's activities, but it felt like a lifetime had passed since they were sitting in my office planning their day on Paradise Island. In a few short hours, I'd been through so much with them. What had happened with Phillip made me think about the lifeguard who saved my life all those years ago. Had he felt the same rush of adrenaline as he swam out to pull a stranger from the violent ocean? He risked his own life every day to save people, and that day he succeeded.

My experience today wasn't as dramatic. I didn't have to fight through a dangerous ocean current to rescue Phillip, but it was intense. The pressure of all those people watching me, waiting for his water-filled lungs to clear so he could breathe again. I didn't think I'd ever felt so many different emotions at one time. As the hours passed, I relived those moments over and over again in my head, and admittedly I was terrified. Mostly because of what might happen next and how it would affect my future.

I hadn't done anything that would cause me to be fired, but what if the company wanted to do everything they needed to in order to protect their reputation? One staff member was certainly disposable to keep their name clear from scandal. There was no doubt in my mind that I was finished if the Edwards decided to sue Epic Cruise Line. I didn't know if they'd have any grounds, but it was still a concern.

Regardless, Josie wasn't just another guest to me after today. We had a history, and now we'd be connected forever. I'd held her husband's life in my hands, and although it hadn't turned out the way we'd hoped, I'm sure she'd never forget me after all of this was over, and I definitely wouldn't forget her.

"Phil was always a go-getter," Drew said, shaking his head. He'd been talking about his brother, but I hadn't been listening. "It didn't matter what it was, he went after it. Whether it was with sports, colleges, and then his media company. My brother did whatever it took to achieve his goals."

I recalled Bobby saying something along the same lines about Phillip, except he hadn't made it sound as admirable. I thought about mentioning this to Josie and Drew, but it wasn't the right time. It was nice talking to them, but I needed to check in with Jack. I was relieved Josie didn't blame me for not saving Phillip. And as much as I wanted to go and hide somewhere, I couldn't avoid the situation any longer. I'd have to face whatever was coming, and most likely it wasn't going to be good.

I was about to leave when Jack and an officer arrived at the St. Thomas Room. Jack gave me a concerned look, which made me feel very uneasy.

"Hello, Ms. Walker, I'm Detective LeFleur. I'll be the lead on the Phillip Edwards case."

"Hello," I said as I tried to ignore the lump that was forming in my throat.

The detective was tall and slender with jet black hair and had one of the deepest voices I'd ever heard. He immediately led Drew away to speak to him privately, leaving Jack and me with Josie. We all knew a full investigation was coming, but it made me nervous knowing it was official.

"Mrs. Edwards, on behalf of Epic Cruise Line, please accept our deepest condolences on the passing of your husband," Jack said, holding out his hand.

She shook it before dabbing the corners of her eyes. She hadn't shed any tears since earlier in our conversation. "I appreciate that very much. Phillip and I were really looking forward to our celebration cruise." She cleared her throat. "I can't believe he's gone." She continued to hold it together, but I noticed her gaze move to where Drew and the detective were still talking. Not that I blamed her—I was also very curious about their conversation.

"Yes, I understand," Drew said as he and the detective walked back to us. He looked even more upset than before, which made my heart sink.

"What's going on?" Josie asked, her voice shaking slightly.

Drew patted her on the shoulder. "The police are putting a rush on the tests. They want to nail down his exact cause of death and find out what substances were in his system."

She frowned. "What do you mean? They already know he had a lot to drink. We were all celebrating, but he didn't seem intoxicated to the point of passing out."

Detective LeFleur shook his head. "Not just alcohol, Mrs. Edwards."

She narrowed her eyes. "Wait. Other substances? What exactly are you saying? Phillip didn't do drugs."

He nodded. "Mr. Edwards' parents had the same reaction. After his body was examined by the coroner, there were some signs indicating that he ingested a drug or poison. Of course, the reports will show what exactly was in his system. Your in-laws want to know exactly how their son died, and it's my job to find out the truth."

"Poison? What signs?" I asked. I tried to think back to when I pulled him out of the water, but I'd been so focused on trying to get him to breathe. He'd had the normal signs of someone who'd been underwater. I remember noticing his face was a bit red, but I assumed that was from the water temperature in the hot tub.

The detective's calm demeanor didn't change. "Size of pupils and redness of skin to name a few. We have to look into every possibility."

My imagination started to take over. Wow. What if Phillip had been drugged? The idea made me sick to my stomach, but what if it really wasn't an accident?

"We're trying to establish a timeline," the detective continued, dragging me away from my thoughts. "We need to find out who the last person was with Phillip before he got into the hot tub and the amount of time he was there before you and Ms. Walker found him."

Josie's face turned pale, and she slowly dropped down onto the couch. "Well, I was with him earlier. We were discussing some family stuff, and I got frustrated so I took a walk to clear my head. I walked down to the beach and then returned to the pool. That was when Lexi and I met up."

The detective glanced at Drew and then wrote something in his notebook. "Do you know if anyone else was with him after you left for your walk?" Detective LeFleur asked.

"No. I mean, I don't know," Josie said worriedly.

The detective continued to make notes.

"Phillip's parents do think someone did this to him, don't they?" she asked as her voice shook. "They're going to blame me no matter what, I know it."

"Josie…" Drew said. I could see that he was trying to comfort her, but he looked just as frustrated about what was happening as I was.

While I watched the scene unfold, I thought about what Bobby, Kelsey, and even Josie had told me about Phillip's parents' concerns. It was like something out of a movie. Could Josie be the new doting wife who married for fortune and then killed her husband? Or could it be a friend with a vendetta? I knew this stuff happened in real life, but I never in a million years thought I'd ever see it play out. If Phillip's death wasn't an accident, why would someone he loved want to hurt him? I needed to tell the detective about the argument I'd overheard between Phillip and Kelsey, but I didn't want to add to Josie's pain at that moment. I had to pull him aside away from her. At least for now.

I felt a hand grab my elbow, which caused me to jump about three feet in the air. "Let's talk outside," Jack whispered into my ear.

I followed him out of the room without saying a word. As I walked, I mentally prepared myself for what he'd say to me. I knew I'd become too wrapped up in this, and by extension Epic Cruise Line now was.

"What a mess," I said, rubbing my temples. "My heart is breaking for these people."

"It's very sad," Jack agreed. "I wish there were something more we could do to help Mrs. Edwards. We also have to figure out how to handle it if we need to do damage control."

I chewed on my bottom lip. I knew it was his job to look out for the cruise line, but did he have any compassion for Phillip's wife and brother?

"Did you even mean what you said to Josie when you offered your condolences?"

He furrowed his eyebrows. I was probably overstepping my boundaries with him, but he was being so unemotional. "Of course I did. It's a horrible tragedy, but we also have to be careful just in case you get dragged in any further."

I knew he was referring to my involvement in those final seconds of Phillip's life.

"I don't know, Jack. Something in my gut is telling me this could be more than an accident."

He shoved his hands into his pockets and tightened his jaw. "I understand that, which is why I'm concerned."

I sighed. "Well, from what I've heard, Phillip was having issues with a lot of people. What if someone did this to him and they're setting Josie up to take the blame? None of Phillip's family or friends wanted him to marry her."

I paused while I thought about the random conversations I'd had throughout the day. First with Kelsey and then later with Bobby after Phillip's death. I knew Bobby was drunk, but I'd always heard people were the most honest while they were drinking because they didn't have the same inhibitions. Not to mention it was always easier to talk to strangers. Bobby had been an open book and wanted to get his frustrations off his chest.

"If you have important information, you need to share it with Detective LeFleur." He paused. "I also understand how difficult this must be for you too. And you're handling it very well."

I couldn't help but feel so grateful that he was here. There was something intoxicating and reassuring about Jack. Maybe it was the authoritative side, or maybe I was feeling alone and vulnerable in the moment. It was possible the police were on the brink of investigating a murder, and I'd been hanging out with the victim's wife in the minutes leading up to his death. That was a lot to deal with.

"We're going to have to work together to keep the media at bay," Jack said softly. "The detective was adamant about Phillip's family wanting answers, which is understandable. I'd be the same way if I were faced with a situation like this."

I covered my face with my hands. "I was trying to save a man from drowning," I repeated again. I didn't care how many times I had to say it, I would drill this fact into anyone who would listen as long as I needed to.

"I know you were," he agreed. "I truly believe this situation goes beyond you, but unfortunately you're involved."

"Okay, but what happens if it turns out his wife was behind his death and I was with her? Then what?"

He didn't say anything for a few seconds. "That's why we need to fully cooperate with the authorities. Will you tell me everything while we wait for Detective LeFleur to finish talking with Drew and Josie?

I nodded while I gathered my thoughts. I didn't want to leave anything out. There was the argument I'd witnessed between Kelsey and Phillip and everything Bobby had told me. And I needed to tell him about Josie and how distraught she seemed minutes before I jumped into that hot tub.

"Okay," I agreed.

I followed Jack to the concierge desk. He asked if there was an empty meeting room or office where he could counsel with me.

Counsel?

I had to give the guy props. He sounded so professional, and the accent didn't hurt. The woman at the desk gazed at him adoringly and a few seconds later led us to an empty office. She even offered us coffee and water. I couldn't help but be impressed by Jack's ability to work his magic. Inside the office there was a table and three cozy chairs. It was quiet, a perfect place for us to talk without any interruptions.

I sank into the soft, velvety fabric and leaned my head against the back cushion. The stress of the day was beginning to take over. All I wanted was to soak in a hot bath—obviously not in a hot tub. I'd probably never go in one again.

Jack sat down next to me. A slight sense of relief washed over me because for the first time, it actually felt like someone was in my corner. I started off by telling him about Josie introducing Chloe and me to the guests and then Kelsey sitting down with us. "At first I didn't think anything she said was odd, except she clearly doesn't like Josie. She made it sound like she felt excluded and was only invited here because of the relationship her parents have with Phillip's parents. She told us she, Phillip, and Bobby, grew up together."

"Lexi, I'm not understanding what that conversation could have to do with Phillip's death," he interrupted. "A woman feeling excluded because her friend got married is hardly a legitimate reason to kill a man."

"I'm getting there," I said. "You said you wanted to know *everything*."

He paused. "Fair enough. Continue."

I told him about Phillip interrupting our conversation with Kelsey and then describing the argument I overheard between her and Phillip.

"Are you sure you heard her threaten him?" he asked.

"I'm positive. She threatened to tell Josie something, and he called her bluff. Then she got in his face and told him karma would catch up to him and he'd get everything he deserved. That was the last time I saw Kelsey...or Phillip. Well—you know what I mean."

Jack pursed his lips. "Has Josie said anything to you about this girl?"

"Nothing. But right before we found Phillip, she was really upset about something. Supposedly it had to do with Phillip's family. That's when she told me they thought she'd married him for his money. This was after I saw him with Kelsey."

He rubbed his forehead. "So, it's possible this friend of his had some information he didn't want to get out."

I nervously chewed on my lip. "Chloe and I both felt there was more going on between Kelsey and Phillip, more than just family friends. Kelsey was drinking and talked about Josie with so much contempt."

He raised his eyebrows.

"And speaking of contempt, there's also something going on with Phillip's best friend Bobby. You should've heard him. I couldn't imagine talking about my friend the way he spoke about Phillip." I told Jack what Bobby said. "It was disturbing because it seemed like he was glad he'd died, like he thought Phillip deserved it."

Jack was quiet.

"What do you think?" I asked.

He sighed. "Well, to me it appears there's only one common denominator in all of this."

Finally someone agreed with me. "I know. Phillip Edwards wasn't very popular. And after meeting him, I understand why he had strained relationships. He was cold and uptight."

Jack frowned. "That's not what I was thinking, Lexi. The common denominator is your friend Josie."

I opened my mouth to argue, but nothing came out. I couldn't disagree with him. What if I was wrong about Josie? Maybe the truth was right in front of me the whole time. I had to find out who was with Phillip before he went into that hot tub.

How did I get mixed up in this mess? My head was starting to pound.

"Lexi? I know you've been through a lot today," he said. "I can assure you I'll do what I can to help."

Hearing him say that made me feel a tiny bit better. My career, reputation, and whole life hung in the balance. I didn't know what was going to happen, but one thing was for sure: I wasn't going to curl up into a fetal position and wait. I was going to find out how this happened to Phillip Edwards and why.

"Are you ready to talk to Detective LeFleur?" Jack asked.

I thought about it for a few seconds. "Yes, but I need to do something first."

He eyed me curiously. "And that's more important than telling the detective everything you just told me?"

I sat up straight. Now was my chance to prove myself. I'd made a commitment to Epic Cruise Line. I wasn't able to help Phillip, but if Josie were innocent, I was going to do everything I could to help her.

"Can you give me a little bit longer, please? I want to talk to Kelsey."

He groaned. "I don't think it's a good idea for you to run off and bring attention to yourself."

It was possible the detective was still with Josie and Drew. It could be my only chance to talk to Kelsey. "Please, Jack. I told you yesterday how much I cared about my job, the cruise line, and our guests. Please let me prove myself," I begged, leaning toward him. I was close enough that the scent of his cologne filled my nose. His green eyes drew me in as they locked with mine, forcing me to quickly pull back.

"Alright, I'll cover for you."

I exhaled and stood up. "Thank you."

"Under one condition."

I folded my arms tightly against my chest. "Let's hear it."

He rose to his feet and put his hand on my shoulder, causing a jolt to shoot through my body. "You need to be careful."

"I will."

I quickly made my way back to Jack's friend at the concierge desk. It was time I had another chat with Kelsey. The sooner I got some answers, the sooner I'd be able to return to the ship and never look back.

CHAPTER SIX

My heart was pounding against the wall of my chest. Thanks to Jack, the concierge didn't ask any questions and gave me Kelsey's room number. I took a deep breath and knocked on the door of Room 5500. While I waited, I rehearsed what I wanted to say to Kelsey.

There was no answer, so I took another breath and knocked louder a second time.

Still no answer. Crap. I only had a small window of time to attempt to get answers from Kelsey.

I was about to give up when the door finally opened.

Kelsey stood in the doorway wearing one of the hotel's luxurious robes. Her hair was pulled up on top of her head into the same messy bun, and she had on a pair of black-rimmed glasses covering her swollen eyes. I could see she'd been crying. She leaned against the doorframe and folded her arms against her chest.

"Hi, Kelsey, I'm sorry to bother you. Do you remember meeting me earlier? Lexi Walker, with Epic Cruise Line."

She jutted out her chin. "Yes, I remember. Why are you here?"

I tried to swallow the lump that had been in my throat most of the day. What was I supposed to say? I certainly couldn't tell her I was there to ask her if she poisoned Phillip Edwards. I had to think fast. I probably should've thought it through before randomly showing up at her room.

"I'm here on behalf of the cruise line. I was asked to check on the family and friends of Mr. Edwards, since he was a guest on our ship. We want to help out in any way we can."

"I don't need anything," she said. "Thanks for coming by."

She started to close the door, but I held out my arm to stop it. I couldn't let the opportunity go by without at least trying to get information out of her.

"Okay, fine," I said quickly. "There's another reason I'm here. Could we talk for a few minutes?"

Her glasses were sliding down the bridge of her nose, but she didn't fix them. "I'm really not up for visitors right now."

I held up my hands. "I completely understand, and I promise it'll only take a few minutes."

She hesitated but finally held the door open for me to enter her room. I stepped inside and waited for her to close it behind me. She walked into the room, and I quietly followed her.

The room was actually a suite, and it was gorgeous. There was a large sitting room with a balcony that overlooked the sparkling blue ocean and a long hallway that led to a separate bedroom.

Kelsey sat down in a chair, picked up a glass of wine, and took a sip. I noticed a half-empty bottle of Pinot Noir sitting on a side table, and I had no doubt there were more where that one came from. "What do you want to talk to me about?"

I sat on the edge of the couch and cleared my throat. "Well, to begin, I really am here representing the cruise line, and we do want to offer assistance if needed."

"You said that already," she snapped. "Why don't you just get to the point?" She obviously wasn't in the mood for small talk, and I knew my time was limited before she kicked me out of her room.

"Okay, one of the reasons I'm here is to tell you how sorry I am that I couldn't do more to help Phillip. I tried everything, but we got to him too late. I know he was a close friend of yours."

Kelsey pressed her lips together and stared into her wineglass. "I heard you tried to revive him for several minutes, but you couldn't get him breathing again."

I hadn't realized she wasn't there. I was so focused on saving his life, I hadn't stopped to look around at who was watching me. "Oh, were you not at the pool when it happened?"

She bit her lower lip. "I went for a walk because I'd had enough *partying*."

My brain immediately traveled back to her argument with Phillip. I hadn't seen where either of them went after I hurried away.

"That's when I saw the ambulance arrive. I followed them down to the pool, and"—she removed her glasses and wiped her eyes—"I can't believe Phillip's dead. I keep thinking I'm going to wake up and find out it's all a nightmare."

I felt sorry for her like I did Josie, Drew, and their family. I reached over and placed my hand on hers. "I really wish I'd been able to save him. As a lifeguard you commit to saving lives. This has really affected me and probably will forever."

"Me, too."

Should I be asking her questions in the middle of her grief? Maybe it wasn't a good idea to show up at her room and pry information out of her hours after her friend died. Unfortunately, there was no other way to get answers from her.

"Kelsey, can I ask you a question?"

"What?" Her jaw tightened, and I reminded myself that I needed to tread lightly.

"I was told there's an investigation into Phillip's death. Did you know that his parents are questioning the circumstances of his death?"

"Why do you care?"

I frowned. "I was the one who pulled him out of the water. My boss is worried that we could be facing liability issues because I was on the clock and we weren't on the ship. I don't know the Edwards family, and I'm concerned about what I'm up against."

She finished her glass of wine. "You have plenty of reason to be worried. Family means everything to the Edwards. Too bad they were blind when it came to Phillip and his antics."

I cocked my head to the side. "What do you mean?"

She stretched her arms out in front of her. "Phillip could do no wrong in their eyes—well, except marrying Josie," she said with a snort.

There it was again. It was a perfect segue to get more information on Josie.

"That's something else I've been wondering." I cleared my throat. "Why does everyone dislike Josie so much? It's been many years since I've seen her, but she seems like a genuinely good person."

Kelsey frowned. "Exactly how long has it been? The sweet girl act you see isn't reality. She's good at it though. Very good. She only married Phillip to get her hands on his company and his money. She caused so much turmoil for him and his relationships then took him away from everyone." She paused and stared off into space. I could see the anger in her eyes. I didn't have to be a genius to know she was talking about herself.

"What exactly did she do? I'm just trying to understand the dynamics because I actually just came from talking to her and Drew. She seems devastated."

Kelsey frowned. "Didn't you hear what I said? It's all an act."

She dropped her head and dabbed the corner of her left eye. "If only he'd listened, this wouldn't have happened," she wailed. "He chose marrying her over the people who really loved him, and now he's gone."

I sat still while tears slid down her cheeks. I was so confused because she seemed sincere. She clearly cared about Phillip more than she was letting on. Was Chloe right about something going on between Phillip and Kelsey? Did they have an affair? Could that be the secret Kelsey threatened to tell Josie?

"I'm sorry. You two were very close, weren't you?"
But how close?
"Yes, we were." She paused. "Very close."
Hmm…maybe I was finally getting somewhere.
"Kelsey, were you more than childhood friends?"
A painful expression spread across her face. I could almost see the heartache she was going through.

"I told him he'd get everything he deserved, and he did," she said between her sobs. "It was only a matter of time before karma caught up to him."

That was the last thing she'd said to him during their argument. Had she followed through on her threat?

"Karma? What do you mean by 'karma' and 'everything he deserved,' Kelsey?"

She wiped her tears away and stood up. "I don't want to talk about this anymore. You need to go."

I didn't argue. Instead I followed her toward the door. "Please let me know if there's anything else I can do for you," I said, handing her my card.

"Good-bye, Lexi."

I stopped her before she closed the door. "Kelsey, do you think someone intentionally killed Phillip?"

She stared at me through tear-filled eyes. "Your *good* buddy Josie is the reason Phillip's dead," she said before slamming the door in my face.

I stood outside the hotel room and thought about everything Kelsey had said. She'd gone out of her way to make Josie look like the bad guy, and I had no doubt she'd tell the police that. I still didn't know what really happened to Phillip, but I was now convinced there was more to his relationship with Kelsey. Did his death have something to do with their argument? And did Kelsey make good on her threat?

* * *

When I returned to where Jack was waiting for me, Detective LeFleur was with him. My heart sank into my stomach. Had Jack told him where I'd gone?

"Hi. Sorry, I needed to get some air."

Jack looked at the detective. "Detective LeFleur was just telling me we should be able to return to the ship very soon."

That was the best news I'd heard all day. I knew Chloe was probably worried, and I couldn't wait to wash the chlorine grime off. "Thank goodness. I'm so ready to go."

"We appreciate your patience, Ms. Walker. I'm sure you can understand this is an unusual case because Mr. Edwards was a passenger on your ship but passed here at the resort."

I nodded. "I understand, and I'm more than willing to comply with whatever you need."

The detective looked at Jack and back at me. "We already have your statement from the time of death, but I'm trying to get a good grasp on the events of the day. Unfortunately, the preliminary reports are showing that Mr. Edwards ingested some kind of poison."

My heart sank. "Okay."

"I have a few more questions about the time before you came upon Phillip in the hot tub."

I nodded.

"Mrs. Edwards told you there were some problems within the family, isn't that right?"

"Yes."

"Did she mention her husband's business?"

I shook my head. "I don't know anything about his business. The only thing she said was his family didn't think she was good enough for him. She was upset because her in-laws were giving her a hard time."

"You said she was distraught. Can you describe her behavior?"

The events of the day were beginning to run together. I closed my eyes as I tried to picture Josie right before we found Phillip.

"She seemed distracted and anxious. She said Phillip had told her not to worry about their issues, but she couldn't help it. She said she didn't think it would ever get better."

"She said she went for a walk before returning to the pool. Did you see her with anyone else?"

I hesitated. "I'm not exactly sure. I was having another conversation when I noticed her. I could tell she was upset—that's when I approached her."

He stopped asking questions for a minute while he continued making notes. I took a slow deep breath as I tried to calm myself.

"Did you see Phillip and Josie interact at all today? Can you tell me how they acted with one another?"

As I replayed the day in my head, I suddenly realized that I hadn't seen them together. Not one time. The only person I'd seen Phillip interact with was Kelsey.

"I don't remember seeing them. But there's actually something else I think you should know about."

He gave me a curious look. "What's that?"

I looked at Jack, who nodded. "Earlier today I overheard an argument between Phillip and his friend Kelsey. She was yelling at him and threatening to tell his wife something. He blew her off, and she was visibly upset. That was the last time I saw Phillip...until I got him out of the hot tub."

The detective searched through his notepad. "Are you referring to Kelsey Clark?"

I shrugged. "I don't know her last name, but I assume that's her. Apparently her family is very close friends with the Edwards. She told my friend and me that she grew up with Phillip and Bobby."

He jotted something down in his notepad. "Yes. Ms. Clark spoke to one of the officers on the scene immediately following Phillip's death, but I have more questions for her."

Jack nudged me.

"Detective LeFleur, I want to fully cooperate with you. Josie Edwards and the family deserve answers, and I thought this information might help."

"Did Ms. Clark only tell you about the family relationships? Did she say anything else that stood out to you?"

I frowned. "I asked her if she and Phillip were closer than just friends. She said they were. And she talked about Josie."

He continued making notes. "And what did she say?"

Ugh. I was afraid Josie's hole was growing bigger, and I wasn't helping. What was I supposed to do? I couldn't lie to a detective. I had to tell him what I knew. "It was along the same lines, about his family not accepting her and that they all warned him not to marry her."

The detective put the pen cap to his lips. "Have you had any other interactions today?"

I needed to tell him about Bobby. It seemed to me like most of the suspicion had fallen upon Josie. Maybe it was because of the family's negative feelings for her? I wondered if there was a chance she was being set up. And if possible I needed to remind him that my only *recent* connection to the couple was booking their resort experience and trying to save Phillip's life.

"I spoke to Phillip's friend Bobby," I said as I folded my arms against my chest. "I wanted to offer my condolences, but he was rambling about Phillip. It was hard to follow because he was so drunk. Anyway, from the way he was talking, it sounded like he and Phillip were having some issues. He said something about Phillip caring more about success than the people in his life. Honestly, he seemed really mad, and it almost sounded like he thought Phillip deserved this."

Detective LeFleur gave a thoughtful look. "I tried to speak to him, but like you said, he was too inebriated to form a complete sentence. As soon as I'm able to question him, I will. What else did you discuss?"

I sighed. There was nothing I could do. I had to answer his questions honestly. "He told me he was mad because Phillip didn't listen to him when he expressed his concerns about their marriage. Like everyone else, he insisted that they shouldn't have gotten married."

Ugh. I was so nauseated. I felt like I'd made everything worse for Josie. It didn't matter though. Just because her in-laws didn't like her didn't mean she killed her husband.

"You've been extremely helpful, Ms. Walker."

I nodded pensively. "I hope I'm not overstepping here, but I was just thinking—we know Phillip's family and friends didn't accept their marriage, and now he's dead. Josie being involved seems too easy and convenient to me. Again, I just met Phillip for the first time last night and it's been years since I've seen Josie."

Out of the corner of my eye, I noticed Jack staring at me.

"Lexi, our car should be here any minute," Jack stated firmly. He probably wasn't happy with my comment about Josie, but I didn't care. I'd been doing my job and ended up in the wrong place at the wrong time, and I wanted answers.

"I appreciate your opinion on this, Ms. Walker. I've been doing this for eighteen years, and I can assure you I'll do everything I can to get justice for Phillip Edwards."

I was glad to hear that, but I couldn't help but wonder who was looking out for Josie? That's why I wasn't going to give up on finding out the truth one way or another.

CHAPTER SEVEN

———

Jack and I were finally headed back to the ship. Epic Cruise Line had connections with private car companies in most ports. It was nice of Jack to use them instead of a local taxi. Detective LeFleur had told us he had all the information he needed from us for now. Unfortunately, we still had another two days in port, so I had a feeling it wasn't over yet. I stared out the window as we left Paradise Island, making our way back to where the ship was docked. I watched as we drove through the streets lined with colorful architecture. One after another, we passed pink, blue, and orange buildings. Many had fallen into disrepair, and the paint had chipped off some of the structures. There was no doubt that decades of sun, salt, and hurricanes had left their mark, but they still held so much character. It was hard to wrap my head around how much history these streets had seen. I always loved coming to the Bahamas and sharing my love for these island nations with our guests. Unfortunately, there was a feeling of dread still looming after the traumatic events of the day. I was anxious about the questions I faced from my coworkers. Maybe it'd be best to avoid them until I knew more. Hopefully that would be soon.

The detective had told us Josie would be staying at the resort for the night and, depending on the investigation, might return to the ship before we sailed. The cruise line would make arrangements to pack up both Phillip's and her things.

Ugh. I hadn't even thought about all of his things being on our ship.

"You're awfully quiet all of sudden," Jack said, interrupting my daydream. "You certainly weren't while talking to the detective."

I didn't know how to take his comment. Maybe he didn't approve of me asking the detective questions, but I didn't care. I had every right to express my own opinions and concerns.

"I'm very tired. This has been the longest day ever."

"You did a good job, though. You were honest and forthcoming," he added.

Yeah, I was honest, alright. I just worried I'd done more harm than good for Josie, which hadn't been my intention.

"Thanks. I told you I have nothing to hide and wanted the detective to know that, too. I just feel like I need to keep telling everyone that I reconnected with Josie for the first time last night," I said. It didn't hurt to remind him about that little fact either. The last thing I needed was to be labeled as an accomplice in Phillip's death.

He nodded. "I understand. Well, it was certainly an eventful first day for me," he said, leaning his head against the back seat. "I've faced a lot since being in this role, but this was a new experience even for me."

Really? I guess even the very successful Jack Carson wouldn't be prepared for a possible murder scandal. Based on what I'd heard, I would've guessed he'd be an expert in all types of situations. However, murder investigations were probably above his pay grade.

"By the way, I've spoken with your immediate supervisor and made arrangements for you to have some time off. I figured you needed it after today."

I appreciated Jack's help, but I couldn't help but wonder if this time off would be more than temporary. "I think a day off would be helpful. But I'd like to return to work as quickly as possible."

Assuming I still had a job.

"At least in Port Adventures," I added, glancing out of the window as we drove through the tiny island streets.

I wasn't sure what was going to happen to my lifeguard position. I'd probably have to talk to Javier about it. He was the head of the department and a really cool guy. But as nice as he was, the cruise line still had to consider the safety of passengers, and if there were any doubt about my skills, they had to do what was best for them. Hopefully the cause of Phillip's death would reveal that I'd done everything I could to revive him.

"Lexi, it's okay to take some time. You've been through quite an ordeal today."

I let out a sigh of relief as the *Legend* came into view. I'd never been so happy to see it.

"Hopefully they get some answers soon," I said. "I really want to move on from this day."

We pulled up to the dock and got out of the car. Jack and I walked side by side toward the ship. There was a beautiful breeze coming off the ocean, and I could hear loud music coming from the top deck. It was crazy to think about the ship full of people still enjoying their vacations. Josie and Phillip should've been able to do that, too.

"Do the other guests know what happened?" I asked.

Jack shoved his hands into his pockets. "We didn't make any announcements. Unfortunately people talk, and I think news of a drowning is traveling through the ship. Our team has been fielding questions as they arise, but our goal is to keep it as normal as possible for the rest for the passengers."

Good idea. I definitely didn't want everyone to know that one of the ship's lifeguards, namely me, had failed to save a passenger's life.

"Thanks for being there today," I said. "I know it's your job, but it was nice to not have to face it alone."

"I wouldn't have been anywhere else."

We walked in silence for a few seconds before Jack held out his arm to stop me. "Lexi, is there anything I can do for you?"

Let me keep my job?

The glow from the ship lit up the night sky. Jack's sandy brown hair was blowing in the breeze, and even through my exhaustion I felt drawn to him in that moment.

What was wrong with me? A man died on my watch and I was involved in a potential murder investigation, but I was still admiring my boss's boss's boss. He was one hundred percent off-limits, and the most important thing I had to worry about was my reputation.

"Thank you, Jack. All I need right now is a good night's sleep."

He opened his mouth to say something and paused. "So do I. Hopefully we wake up to some good news tomorrow."

I hoped so. I didn't want to go through another day like this ever again.

* * *

After taking the longest shower in the history of mankind, I wrapped the fluffy white towel tightly around my body and brushed through my wet hair. I'd never been so happy to return to my tiny stateroom. Chloe was still doing her show, so I had some time to rest and gather my thoughts before she returned and asked a million questions. I already knew she'd want to hear every detail, and I couldn't blame her. The events of the day were intense compared to our usually quiet sailings. Part of me was actually curious to talk to her, too. I wanted to know what people were saying so I could be prepared for whatever tomorrow would bring.

I pulled my wet hair up into a bun on the top of my head and lay on my bed. As soon as I closed my eyes, I was thrust back into that hot tub. I could almost feel the struggle of pushing Phillip's body out of the water. I sat up straight in my bed and placed my hands over my face. I hoped this wasn't going to be a nightly occurrence. Sleep was one of my favorite things to do, and reliving those terrifying moments over and over could get in the way of that.

Not wanting to close my eyes again, I grabbed a book off my nightstand and tried to immerse myself in the words on the pages—anything to distract myself from the memories.

As I read, my eyes slowly started to close.

* * *

The sound of something buzzing caused me to jump out of bed. I didn't know what time it was, and when I opened my eyes, I noticed Chloe still hadn't returned from her show yet.

It took me a few seconds, but I finally realized the buzzing sound was coming from my Port Adventures phone. I searched through my bag until I located it under my planner. I only used this phone for communications with guests and coworkers, so I was very curious as to who would be calling it.

I had two missed calls from phone numbers I didn't recognize. One must've been a local area code. I immediately wondered if it was Detective LeFleur. I should have saved his number in my phone.

And I recognized the other. It was a 407 area code, which was from Central Florida. My heart sank because those calls must've been important or they wouldn't have called so late.

I dialed the Florida number first, but it went straight to a generic voice mail. I called the local number next and chewed on my fingernail while waiting for an answer.

"It's a glorious day at Paradise Island Resort and Spa. How may I direct your call?"

Someone was calling me from the resort. Maybe it was Josie? I'd given her my card and reminded her to contact me if she needed something. The idea of Josie calling made me feel uneasy. With all the information surrounding Phillip's death coming out, I wasn't sure I wanted to have any more private communication with her.

"Hello, can I help you?" the voice asked.

I cleared my throat. "Yes, I just had a missed call from this number."

"Oh, well, we have hundreds of guests staying on the property. If you know the person who called you, I can transfer you."

Jack's words about my connection with Josie went through my head. There was no way I was asking for her room. "No, thank you. Have a good night."

As I was ending the call, the phone buzzed again. I stared at the flashing number on the screen. It was the resort again.

"Hello?"

"Is this Lexi Walkeerrrr?" a woman slurred.

It wasn't Josie, but I recognized the voice. "Yes, this is Lexi. Who's calling?"

"This is Kelsey Clark. I met youuu today."

Holy crap. Why was Kelsey calling me? I'd given her my card too, but I hadn't expected her to actually use it.

"Hi, Kelsey, are you okay?

Silence.

"Hello, are you still there?"

"I'm here, but you keep cutting out," she whined. By the way she spoke, I assumed she'd finished off her bottle of Pinot and possibly a second one. Of course we had a bad connection. My stateroom was deep inside the ship, so I moved closer to the window.

"Can you hear me better now?" I yelled.

"Yes, much. Lexi, when you came to my room, you told me to call you if I needed to talk."

My curiosity was piqued. *What did she want to talk to me about?*

"Absolutely. What can I do for you?"

"Welllll, I think you asked me a question when you were in my room, and I wanted to answer it."

Seriously? I'd asked her a lot of questions, and I was much too exhausted to remember every detail. Unless she was ready to talk about Phillip? I had to take this opportunity to get as much information out of her as possible.

"Does this have to do with your relationship with Phillip?" I asked.

Silence.

I wondered if she'd passed out. "Kelsey? Are you still there?"

"Yes."

My heart started to race. It was now or never to get her to admit if she knew anything about his death.

"I know you don't know me, but I've always felt like it was easier to talk to strangers. I couldn't help but notice that things seemed intense between you and Phillip at the resort. And I heard you arguing…" I chewed my lip as I waited for her to take the bait. "You loved him, didn't you?" I asked softly. "And you were romantically involved."

I could hear her crying into the phone. "He told—" she shouted.

The phone was cutting out again. "Kelsey, can you repeat that? The phone broke up."

"He told me he loved meeee, but he chose her. Why didn't he choose me?" she yelled into the phone. "It was finally our time, like it was always meant to be. I waited for him, but he broke his promise. I hate her so much. He told me we would be together."

I knew it. They were more than friends. That must've been what she was threatening to tell Josie.

"Kelsey, how long ago was this? Were they already engaged?" I asked.

"It's all her fault. She took him away from meeee," she yelled, ignoring my question. "Do you know how it feels to lose everything? It's the worst feeling everrrr. It wasn't supposed to be this way."

There was nothing I could say to calm her down. I could hear the sadness and the pain in her voice. One thing was for sure… It sounded like Phillip had caused a lot of pain, and these women had to pick up the pieces.

"Phillip was murdered," she shouted. "Don't you seeeee? I told him he'd get what he deserved, and he did. I'll never forgive myself."

Wait, was she admitting that she killed him?

The phone cut out again, and there was silence on the other end.

"Kelsey?"

I looked at the phone screen and noticed the call had failed. Just then the door to my room clicked and Chloe walked in. She looked stunning in her pink halter dress, her hair twisted perfectly on the top of her head. She rushed to hug me as soon as she noticed I'd returned. "Lexi, thank goodness you're back."

I didn't respond, still clutching my phone with my hand.

Chloe gave me a confused look. "Are you alright? You look worried. Did something else happen?"

I didn't answer her because I was trying to decide what to do next. I needed to call the detective, and maybe Jack, to tell them about Kelsey's call. I frantically looked through the contents of my bag in search of Detective LeFleur's information.

Ugh. Again I wondered why I hadn't saved his number. What was I thinking?

"What are you looking for? Can I help?" she asked.

"I need to find the detective's information," I said as I flipped through the pages of my planner. "Kelsey just called me. I gave her my card when I was at the resort. I think she might've been trying to confess," I exclaimed. "And you were right about her and Phillip. She told me about their relationship. Apparently he said he loved her but chose Josie. She was practically hysterical."

Chloe's eyes grew big. "I knew it."

CHAPTER EIGHT

───────

We finally found the detective's info in my wallet, which was exactly where I'd put it for safekeeping. It had been such a long, emotional day—at some point I must've zoned out because I barely remember taking his card. I didn't waste any more time and immediately left two messages for Detective LeFleur about Kelsey's phone call. I thought about calling Jack, but there was nothing he could do at this time of night either. There was no reason to interrupt his sleep, which was what I needed to be doing.

Chloe changed into her pajamas and sat on the bed with me while I updated her on what had happened after she left the resort.

I sighed and stretched out on my bed. "Phillip's family must really despise Josie," I said as I yawned widely. "I still can't believe I run into her after all these years and within twenty-four hours I'm thrust into a family feud and murder investigation."

Chloe gave a thoughtful look. "Lexi, do you think there's a chance she *could* have poisoned him? I mean, she seems lovely, but what if she's just pretending to be that nice? People really do put on facades, you know. I've watched programs about twisted people living normal lives, and no one suspects they've gone mad."

Chloe's suggestion reminded me of what Kelsey said when I was in her room.

"I've wondered the same thing. Kelsey said the person we all see isn't the real Josie. Then she said that Josie took Phillip away from the people who really loved him."

Chloe rolled her eyes. "I'm guessing what she meant was Josie took him away from *her*. Of course she's going to say that.

She's bitter because Phillip married another woman. I could see her jealousy from a mile away. She was giving Josie the death stare."

"I wonder how recent their affair was," I said. "Could you imagine if it happened right before the wedding?" I cringed at the thought. "I heard Kelsey threaten Phillip about going to Josie with the truth. He was so nasty to her. He actually said no one cared what she had to say. I felt sorry for her then, but now I don't know what to think."

Honestly, I didn't understand what these women saw in Phillip Edwards. I didn't think he was friendly at all, and based on what other people had said about him, my first impression seemed pretty accurate.

I glanced at the time. It was after one o'clock. I doubted the detective would call me back tonight.

"I'm so confused, Chloe," I said. "On one hand I'm really worried about my job with the cruise line. At the same time I feel this overwhelming responsibility to help Josie and get justice for Phillip because I failed to save him."

She put her hand on my shoulder. "That's a lot of pressure to put on yourself."

I massaged my temples. "I keep going over all these different scenarios in my head. I overheard her tell him she hoped karma would catch up to him, and then she admitted it to me. Of course, I left before they saw me, so I don't know if anything else happened between them. Regardless, I never saw Phillip after that until we found him in the hot tub."

Chloe yawned as I rambled on.

"I'm sorry, Chloe. I need to let you get some sleep, and I should probably try as well."

She shook her head. "I'm fine. Finish what you were saying."

I hesitated but continued. "I'm almost done, I promise. I was just thinking about how upset Kelsey was, and who knows how long this relationship had been going on. I asked her, but she didn't tell me. Maybe she finally snapped and she drugged him. On the other hand, I also wonder if Josie somehow found out about Phillip and Kelsey, or maybe she knew all along."

I paused. "It's just all so overwhelming, and I'm completely baffled by the strange relationships between these people. How could Bobby be so cold and callous after a death of a friend? I'd be beside myself if something happened to anyone I cared about."

Chloe gave me a sympathetic look. "Lexi, I think you should get some rest or you're going to drive yourself mad. It isn't your job to solve this case."

I sighed loudly. "You're right. But what if my past connection to Josie plays a factor in the investigation? You watched me try to resuscitate him, but Phillip's parents weren't here to see how hard I tried. They can only go off of the witness accounts that I did everything I could."

"You had no reason not to save him," she insisted. "The fact that they don't like their daughter-in-law has nothing to do with you."

I appreciated Chloe's efforts of trying to calm me down. Hearing her say it helped a lot. Unfortunately, I became involved the second I met with Josie and Phillip and got in even deeper when I dragged Phillip out of that water. Receiving those frantic calls from Kelsey tonight made a complicated situation even worse. Maybe it wasn't the smartest idea to confront her. Jack might've been right after all.

"I know, Chloe. It's just difficult to think about anything else."

"I understand, but it's been a terribly long day," she said, pulling back her bed comforter. "You'll have a fresh start tomorrow. For now you need to take care of you."

She was right. I needed to try to relax, and there was nothing else I could do tonight. I finally crawled into bed. Unfortunately, despite being exhausted, I was wide awake. I wished I could shut my brain off, but instead I stared at the ceiling.

"Did you spend a lot of time with Jack Carson today?" Chloe asked a few minutes later.

I laughed. Now that was a typical Chloe question. We were in the middle of a murder investigation, and she wanted to know if I'd spent time with a man.

"I thought you were asleep?"

She giggled. "Nearly. But it just occurred to me that I left you alone with him at the resort all day. Did he comfort you?"

"Alone? Not quite. Yes, I was with Jack—plus a detective, police officers, some reporters, and hundreds of vacationers."

"Lexi, it's a proven fact that emotional and intense situations bring people together."

I sighed loudly. "Whether it's true or not, let me remind you that he's super high-up in our company, which makes him a big no-no for me. Therefore I won't be having *alone* time with Jack, at least not in the way you're talking about."

"Fine, I get your point. Good night."

I hoped she'd let it go, but Chloe was a hopeless romantic. I purposely hadn't told her about the reaction I had when Jack touched me, because I'd never have heard the end of it.

I had much bigger issues to worry about than being attracted to Jack Carson.

CHAPTER NINE

———

"Lexi, wake up."

I felt a cold hand shaking my arm. *What's happening? Where am I?* It felt like I'd just fallen asleep.

"Lexi, come on."

When I finally opened my eyes, Chloe was standing over me.

"Your phone has been ringing nonstop," she whined, still half asleep. "Can you answer it or turn it off? I need to get more sleep."

My phone?

The memories of the day before crept in, including Kelsey's strange phone call. I hopped up and reached for my phone while Chloe hobbled back to her bed. She pulled the covers up to her neck, covered her eyes with her night mask, and rolled over.

"Sorry," I whispered.

It was barely seven o'clock, and I tried desperately to hold my eyes open as I listened to my voice mails. The first was from the detective, confirming he'd received my message and would follow up. The second call was from Jack, apologizing for bothering me but asking if I could stop by his office at my earliest convenience.

Hearing his voice caused a stir inside me.

As much as I wanted to stay in bed, I didn't waste any time in getting ready for my day. If I'd lain back down, I probably wouldn't have gotten up for hours. I had no idea what to expect today, but I needed to look as put together as possible.

After a quick shower to help me get moving, I chose a light pink silk blouse and paired it with dark black skinny jeans.

At least I'd look better than I had yesterday, thanks to my unexpected jaunt in the hot tub. I added a few loose beachy waves to my hair and applied some makeup to cover the dark circles under my eyes. The reflection in the mirror showed how tired I was, but this was the best I could do on only four hours of sleep.

Very quietly I snuck out of the room so I didn't disturb Chloe. I felt guilty about her being stuck at the resort with me yesterday. Thankfully she was an understanding friend. I definitely got lucky with her. Chloe was my fourth roommate in the two years I'd been with Epic Cruise Line, and she'd been the best by far. My other roommates had been messy, mean, and thieves—in that order.

I was so happy when Chloe joined our staff five months ago. We'd actually met on one of our sister ships last year and hit it off right away. I immediately saw that she was fun and energetic. Over time I learned that she was one of the kindest people I'd ever met.

My previous roommate, who was also in the entertainment department, had just been fired for getting into a fight with a group of guests when Chloe's act had moved to our ship. It was the best day ever.

I took a few deep breaths and plastered a friendly smile on my face as I made my way toward the executive offices. I wasn't sure where Jack's office was located since he'd just arrived on the ship a few days earlier. As soon as I walked in I saw Anabelle, one of the ship officers' assistants, sitting at the front desk.

She pursed her lips as soon as she saw me. "Lexi, how are you doing today?"

"I'm fine, just a little tired."

"It's so sad what happened to that poor man. How's his wife?"

Anabelle had a reputation for gossiping, so she was the last person I'd talk to about my experience. "I'm not sure. I'm actually here to meet with Jack Carson."

She motioned for me to follow her and thankfully didn't ask any more questions.

As soon we turned the corner, she led me to an open door, where Jack was sitting at a desk, typing on a laptop. He stood and waved me in as soon as he saw me. There wasn't much set up in his office yet. Of course, he had been busy since arriving on the *Legend*. Maintaining the stellar reputation of our cruise line took precedence over decorating.

"Good morning, Lexi."

Anabelle pulled the door closed behind me, leaving Jack and me alone.

"Morning. I'm sorry it took me so long. I had a hard time falling asleep last night."

I nervously shifted from one foot to the other.

"I understand. Fortunately, I was out the second my head my head hit the pillow."

Jack looked very refreshed, despite our long day. He was wearing a crisp gray shirt, black slacks, and no tie. His green eyes were magnified behind a pair of square-framed glasses. The glasses were a good look for him, not that he needed them, because he looked as handsome as the day before. Men had it so much easier. As stressful as yesterday had been for us, looking at Jack, you'd never have known it.

He finally returned to his seat, so I sat down in one of the empty chairs.

"Detective LeFleur reached out to me this morning," he said.

I sucked in a breath. "Yes. I left him a message last night after receiving a disturbing phone call from Kelsey." I paused. "I would've called you, but it was practically the middle of the night."

He nodded. "I appreciate that. I need a lot of sleep, otherwise I'm a bear to be around. Getting enough rest helps me keep a clear head in all situations."

I wished I had gotten more rest. I felt like I'd been hit by a truck.

"So, what did Detective LeFleur say?" I asked, changing the subject.

He took his glasses off and pressed his hands together with his fingers touching. "Well, to begin with, they got the results back from the lab. They found high levels of Rohypnol in Phillip's system."

The news caused the hair on the back of my neck to stand up. *Roofies? Wasn't that the stuff people put in drinks?* As selfish as it sounded, I immediately wondered if those results meant I was in the clear. If he'd been drugged and then drowned—there was probably nothing I could have done to help him after all.

Jack must have noticed my discomfort. "I know this is unsettling," he continued after clearing his throat. "Detective LeFleur also said he was going to speak to Kelsey regarding your phone call."

I nodded as I tried to gather my thoughts.

"I, um, want to tell him everything Kelsey said before he speaks to her."

Jack picked up his phone and scrolled. "We can try to catch him now."

He put his phone on speaker and placed it on the desk. As we waited for the detective to answer, I looked around the empty office. There were no pictures other than a framed cover of *Vacation Sensation* magazine lying on the corner of his desk. There wasn't anything personal other than a laptop, some folders, and a plain white coffee cup.

I was a little curious about Jack as a person. Obviously I knew all about his career and his favorite football team.

Detective LeFleur's phone went to voice mail.

"I really hope he's able to fill in the gaps by talking to Kelsey."

"What did she say?" Jack asked. "And why did she call you in the first place?"

I sighed. "I gave her my card yesterday when I was at the resort. And I was trying to get some information out of her, so I suggested that sometimes it's easier to talk to strangers than people we know."

Jack raised his eyebrows. "Okay."

"Anyway, I'm pretty sure she was drunk, because she was slurring her words. I saw the half-empty wine bottle in her room yesterday, and I doubt she stopped drinking after I left." I paused as I recalled the details of our conversation. "I told her I had overheard her argument with Phillip, and I asked her about their relationship. She admitted that he told her he loved her but then chose to marry Josie. She was hysterical—it was obvious Phillip had broken her heart."

"So why is she here? Why would she come to the Bahamas to see the man she loves with another woman?" he asked, folding his hands in front of him.

"Phillip asked her the same thing during their argument," I said. "She told Chloe and me that she came because their families had been close for years, and therefore Phillip and Bobby were stuck with her."

I chewed on my lip as her desperate words played through my mind.

"The last thing she said before the phone cut out was that Phillip was murdered."

Jack raised his eyebrows.

"She said she'd never forgive herself because she'd wished it on him."

My mind began to flip through possible scenarios. Kelsey didn't admit to killing Phillip, but she blamed Josie for everything. Was she saying Josie did it, or did she just want me to think she did?

"Lexi?"

Jack's voice snapped me out of my daydream. "Sorry. I was just sorting through everything in my mind. Now we know he had Rohypnol in his system, he had strained relationships with Kelsey and Bobby, and he was involved with Kelsey at some point and broke her heart. And no one close to him was supportive of his marriage."

Jack rubbed his forehead vigorously.

"Are you okay?" I asked.

Jack sighed. "I'm sorry. I'm afraid I'm a bit on edge."

He's on edge? He certainly did a good job of hiding it. In his defense, a potential scandal for the cruise line would be unnerving for the director of public relations.

"Trust me, I know the feeling," I replied.

The sound of Jack's phone ringing made me jump.

"Hello, Detective."

My ears perked up, and I immediately wondered if he'd spoken to Kelsey yet. I stayed quiet while Jack spoke to him.

"Lexi is here in my office. She wanted to speak to you before you spoke with Kelsey." He put the phone on speaker and laid it down on his desk.

"Hello," I said absently. "I'm sorry I called so late last night. I didn't know what to do." I listened as he asked me to recall the conversation I'd had with Kelsey. I explained that we'd had a bad connection and the call got cut off, but she eventually admitted to having an affair with Phillip. "She kept repeating how Josie had taken Phillip away from her and then mentioned her argument with him. The last thing she said to me was that he was murdered."

I glanced at Jack, who was watching me.

"Did she give any explanation to her statement or say who she thought was responsible?" the detective asked. His voice was even deeper over the phone.

"No, it was difficult to follow her because she was so upset, and the slurring didn't help. It's safe to assume she was highly intoxicated. The call dropped, and she never called me back."

"Detective LeFleur, is there anything you need us to do?" Jack added. "As I said yesterday, you have the full support of Epic Cruise Line."

"Not right now, but I'll keep you updated," he said. "Thank you, Ms. Walker."

When the call ended, Jack looked up at me. "Alright, I guess we wait now."

I wasn't sure if Kelsey would be as open with the detective as she'd been with me. I still wondered if she was just being overly dramatic because Phillip hadn't reciprocated her feelings. He wasn't alive to give his side of the story, so all we had to go on was her version. After everything I'd learned, I had no idea what to believe.

"I feel like there are so many layers to this situation," I blurted out. "A sudden death, strained friendships, a jilted lover with a broken heart, a complicated family relationship, and a forbidden marriage. I feel like we've fallen into a movie."

One corner of Jack's mouth curled up into a smile. "It does seem that way. You really do pay attention to detail. I respect that about you, Lexi."

I relaxed my shoulders a little.

"While I was on the last ship, we had a situation occur where a staff member had an encounter with a guest," he explained.

I raised my eyebrows. "Really? What happened?"

Jack pressed his fingers together. "It got ugly. Long story short, the wife caught her husband with the staff member, and she went ballistic. I had to do a lot of damage control because even though it was an individual's poor choice that caused the issue, she was still a representative of Epic Cruise Line. Our guest was angry and wanted someone to blame."

I knew where he was going with his story. Drew had told us his parents were grieving, and they needed to direct their anger at someone. Of course, most of their anger seemed to be directed at Josie. She and I had a history, and I was the one who'd tried and failed to revive their son.

Jack shifted around in his seat. "Lexi, please don't take this wrong."

Ugh. It was never good when someone said those words.

"While I admire your determination, you're not a detective. Perhaps leaving it up to the authorities from here on out would be the best idea."

I sighed. "I understand what you're saying, but I'm still concerned about what Drew Edwards told us. What if his parents really are looking for a reason to blame Josie? She and I found Phillip in the hot tub. There's probably nothing I could have done to save him, but what about guilty by association?" I paused as I tried to collect myself. "I'm just going through the possibilities. I know the cruise line would want to distance itself from any negative publicity, and I respect that."

Jack laced his fingers together and stared at me with his gorgeous green eyes. I found myself staring back. Why did he have to be so attractive?

"Very interesting."

"What?" I asked.

"You surprise me."

I wasn't sure if it was a good surprise or not. Hopefully it was good and he saw my work ethic.

"Is that a good thing?"

Our eyes locked again, and I felt the same familiar jolt as the night before when we were walking on the dock. Ugh. *What was I doing?*

"It's—" His phone rang loudly, interrupting what he was about to say. Someone had lousy timing. He held up one finger, hopefully letting me know he'd finish what he was saying.

"This is Jack Carson."

He furrowed his eyebrows.

"What? When?"

Suddenly all the color drained from his face, which made me uneasy.

"Yes. Hold on."

He put the phone down on his desk and placed his hand to his forehead. He had an empty expression on his face. It was obvious that the information he had just received wasn't good.

"Go ahead," he said loudly after putting the phone on speaker.

A lump was already forming in my throat. I had no idea what the call was about, but I had a really bad feeling.

"Ms. Walker, this is Detective LeFleur again. Sadly, we weren't able to speak to Ms. Clark."

My stomach suddenly felt hollow, and my pulse was racing. "Why?"

"Her body was just found. Shockingly enough, she was in a hot tub."

The next few seconds went by in a blur. I felt like I was a million miles away after hearing those words. I'd just spoken with Kelsey hours before, and now she was gone? Was it a coincidence she died in a hot tub? Something told me it wasn't.

"What happened to her?" I asked. "Do you think someone did this to her or—" I paused as I thought about the other possibility. "Or did she kill herself? She was completely distraught on the phone."

Jack reached across his desk and put his hand on mine. I appreciated his gesture.

"The preliminary reports are showing there may have been a struggle."

"How do you know for sure?" I insisted.

"We have our reasons, Ms. Walker," he said. I detected a bit of annoyance in his voice. Maybe he didn't like all my questions, but I didn't care.

Jack must've picked up on it too because he grabbed his phone and turned off the speaker.

I couldn't move as I tried to make sense of what I'd just heard. My mind raced with thoughts about the sad situation and why this had happened. The first thing that came to my mind was the state Kelsey was in the night before. Had the guilt or overwhelming grief taken over? Was it possible the same person killed both Phillip and Kelsey, and was it revenge for their betrayal? Maybe Josie had found out what happened between the two of them after all. There were so many possibilities, and none of them were good.

I felt a hand touch my shoulder, which pulled me out of my thoughts. Jack was now standing beside me.

"Lexi, we need to go over to the resort," he said softly. "I know I told you to take the day off."

I shook my head. "I understand. I'm just in shock right now."

Selfishly, I couldn't help but wonder if I was the last person to talk to Kelsey. I was grateful I'd been here on the ship last night and far away from that hot tub. If Kelsey's family were anything like Phillip's, they were going to want justice for their child and would stop at nothing to get it.

"Why don't you go to your room and take a few minutes? I have to follow up on a few things and then we can head out. Have you had breakfast yet?"

I stood up from my chair. "Not yet. I could use a cup of coffee." *With a shot of something stronger.* I didn't say that out loud, though. I could use a drink or three after hearing the latest news, but I needed to be on top of things now more than ever.

"Get some breakfast, and we'll meet at the gangway in an hour." He led me to the door and opened it for me.

"Thank you," I said, forcing a smile.

He shook his head. "No need. This is why I'm here."

As nervous as it made me, I was grateful he was.

I was about to step out of his office when Jack put his arm out to stop me. I turned to look at him, my forced smile beginning to fade. He must've noticed my expression change, because he put his hands on my shoulders, which was both awkward and wonderful. It wasn't exactly intimate, but it was reassuring. In that moment, I didn't feel so alone.

"Hey now, try not to worry. I'm sure this will all be resolved soon. Detective LeFleur and his team are hard at work trying to get it figured out."

I chewed on my lower lip. "I know. I was hoping today would be a better day, but now it sounds like it may be worse." I wanted to ask him about my status with the cruise line. I was especially worried about my position on the lifeguard staff after what had happened yesterday. It probably wasn't the right time though, and my head was still spinning from the news of Kelsey's sudden death.

I continued to fight back the tears that were threatening to pour out of my eyes. As a member of the Port Adventures team, rising to the occasion and handling unexpected issues was a huge part of my responsibility. That being said, I refused to do the ugly cry in front of Jack Carson.

I cleared my throat. "I think I'll get some breakfast. See you soon."

CHAPTER TEN

———

After grabbing a cup of coffee and a blueberry muffin, I rushed back to my room. I had no appetite, but the caffeine was imperative. Chloe was probably still asleep, but I needed to talk to someone. Our room was dark when I returned, and I immediately felt guilty about waking my poor roommate up again.

I was about to grab my handbag and leave when she rolled over.

"Lexi?"

"Sorry I woke you. I was trying to be quiet," I whispered. "I need to get my stuff for the day, and I'll be out of here."

She stretched her arms high above her head. "It's okay. What are you doing up, anyway? I thought you had the day off?"

Me, too.

I sat on the edge of my bed and took a sip of my coffee. "I'm not exactly working, but I have to go back to the Paradise Island Resort with Jack." I paused and thought about those words. I didn't want Chloe to get the wrong idea. "Well, we're going together, but not like you think. Something terrible happened this morning."

Chloe sat up and turned on the light. "Are you serious? Now what?"

I sighed. "Well, the tests they ran revealed that Phillip had Rohypnol in his system."

She shook her head. "Oh wow. Although I'm not surprised by this news, it's still terrible."

I pressed my lips together as I tried to force the lump out of my throat. "There's more."

She raised her eyebrows. "What do you mean?"

I sighed. "The detective was going to question Kelsey about the phone call we had last night, but they found her body before he could talk to her."

Chloe gasped. "No. What happened?"

"They found her in a hot tub." Just saying those words made me sick to my stomach. How could that have happened not once but twice?

"You're kidding? Did she drown, or was she...?"

I shook my head. "I don't know any details, but the detective said the preliminary results are showing signs of a struggle."

"So why do you have to go back to the resort?" she asked, rubbing her eyes. "You weren't even there."

"I wasn't, but I had a conversation with her last night." I paused. "I might've been the last person she spoke to."

Chloe jumped out of bed. "What time are you going? I'll hop into the shower."

I tried to stop her. "I appreciate it, but I'm not dragging you into this anymore. I'm fully prepared for whatever questions come at me." Although I'd have loved for Chloe to be there with me, I was expecting another long day, and she had to work later that night. It wouldn't do either of us any good for her to draw more attention to herself.

"You shouldn't have to go through this alone," she called from the bathroom. I heard the faucet turn on, and a few seconds later she came out with a toothbrush. "They're going to ask you every detail about the phone call you had with Kelsey, and what if they bring up your friendship with Josie? How much do you want to bet she's their number one suspect now? Her husband was involved with this girl."

I groaned. I had already thought the same thing.

Chloe vigorously brushed her teeth while I tried to come up with a good excuse for her not to come with me. "You're an awesome friend for offering to come with, but I think I'll be fine. Jack will be there, and he's locked and loaded with a plan to defend the cruise line if need be."

Chloe rinsed her mouth. "Is he prepared to defend the cruise line, or you?"

I chewed on my lip as I thought about us on the dock last night and then his reassurance in his office earlier that morning. I hoped he was ready to defend both of us. "It'll be okay. Don't you have rehearsals today?"

She shrugged. "I can blow them off. You, my friend, are more important."

I patted her on the arm. "Thanks. But I got this."

By the time I finally convinced her to let me go on my own, it was time to meet up with Jack. I took a few slow breaths as I walked down the stairwell toward the gangway. When I arrived, Jack was already waiting for me. He'd rolled up his sleeves and was now wearing a pair of aviator sunglasses. Despite being a ball of stress, I couldn't help but notice how good he looked. We scanned our Epic Cruise Line ID cards, and I followed him to the car that was waiting for us.

"You ready to do this?"

I swallowed. "Definitely."

We crawled into the back seat, and the driver shut the door behind us. As we drove toward Paradise Island, I looked back at the ship, wishing I were still on board. I couldn't wait for this sailing to be over.

* * *

I stared out the window as we pulled into the long circular driveway—the Paradise Island Resort looked as grand as ever. Tall white pillars and palm trees lined the road leading up to the main building, and the closer we got, the more nervous I became. It looked like business as usual for the hotel, despite the unfortunate incidents that had occurred within the last day. The valets were busy unloading suitcases and directing traffic. There were guests coming and going, and I noticed a few reporters still milling around.

"Does the media know about all of this?" I asked, still looking out the window.

"Of course," Jack said. "It's their job to find a story. People gossip, and a *drowning* death of a cruise ship passenger is news."

"It's terrible," I said. "Two people have died, and these reporters can't let their family and friends grieve in peace. Can the hotel do something about them being here?"

"Unfortunately not. They have to stay outside, but they can be here as long as they aren't disturbing anyone."

The car pulled up to the front and stopped in front of the grand entryway. A thin valet opened the door, and I stepped out onto the marble-tiled entryway. For a brief moment, I actually felt like I was a high-profile guest instead of a cruise ship lifeguard who'd found a body.

As a few reporters walked toward us, Jack placed his hand on my lower back and quickly led me toward the huge glass doors. I appreciated him being protective of me, even if his intentions were to protect the cruise line.

"Do they know who we are?" I whispered.

"I'm not sure."

When we were safely inside, I spotted Detective LeFleur talking to two men in suits who I assumed were hotel staff. He held up his hand as soon as he saw us. That familiar anxious feeling returned as he walked toward us. My heart was thumping, and my stomach twisted into knots.

"Thanks for coming today," he said. He shook our hands, and I wondered if he was taken aback by my sweaty palms. My nerves had kicked into full gear.

Detective LeFleur led us to a meeting room. I was curious to see if Josie would be there. I had no doubt they were keeping a very close eye on her, especially now after Kelsey's death.

"Can I get you something to drink?" Detective LeFleur asked.

"Yes, please," I replied. My mouth was dry, and I was feeling a little light-headed. I guess I should've finished my muffin after all.

Detective LeFleur produced a bottle of water and handed it to me. I downed half the bottle in one sip.

"What exactly happened with Kelsey?" I asked after clearing my throat.

The three of us sat down, and I folded my hands neatly in my lap.

"Ms. Clark was found by a hotel staff member who was preparing to open one of the recreational spaces. It was not the same recreation area where Phillip Edwards was found. That area is still closed."

Okay, that was my main question. The thought of her dying in the same hot tub really freaked me out. It was still creepy, but at least it wasn't the same place.

"Her hotel room has been searched, and your card was found. We found three empty bottles of wine, so she must have been on a bender. There were no signs that anyone else was in her room with her. What time did you speak to her, Ms. Walker?"

I grabbed my phone from my bag and scrolled through my calls. "It was right before midnight," I said. "I remember thinking it was too late to call you both, but I ended up leaving a message anyway because I was worried."

He opened his notepad. "I made some notes about the call when I spoke to you earlier, but can you recall anything else you think was important from the conversation? Be as specific as possible."

I let out a deep sigh.

"My room is deep in the ship, so reception can be spotty at times. Like I told you before, that made it difficult to have a full conversation. She was very upset—crying, rambling, and she wasn't making a lot of sense. The last thing she said was that he'd been murdered, and then the call dropped."

"Did she admit to killing Phillip Edwards?" he asked.

"Not exactly."

"Did she accuse someone else?"

I paused as I tried to remember Kelsey's exact words. I didn't want to give him the wrong information. "She told me she hated Josie and that it was her fault he died, but she didn't say Josie killed him." I cleared my throat. "Like I said, it was difficult to follow what she was saying."

I looked at Jack, who gave me a thumbs-up. One thing was for sure—despite what was happening, I felt more secure about Jack's opinion of me. He'd been patient and supportive, and I was glad to be here with him.

"Yes, we've already spoken with Mrs. Edwards this morning," he said, not looking up from his notes. "Did you see Kelsey interact with anyone else the day Phillip Edwards died?"

I shook my head. "No. Josie introduced my friend and me to her, but there was a group standing around. Kelsey sat down to talk to us, but she seemed to keep to herself most of the day. The only other person I saw her with was Phillip when they had that argument."

The detective quietly flipped through his notes.

"Can I ask you another question?"

He looked up and smirked. "Of course. I expected you would."

Out of the corner of my eye, I saw Jack wince. Maybe I asked a lot of questions, but too bad.

"You said there appeared to be a struggle?" I asked. "Do you still think it's possible that Kelsey drugged Phillip and then took her own life? She said she'd never forgive herself for wishing something bad would happen to him."

He flipped through his notepad.

"Ms. Clark was fully clothed, and there were scrapes on her arms. It appeared that she was trying to get out of the hot tub. It's possible someone was holding her underwater. The area is closed off as we conduct a detailed search."

I shuddered at the thought of someone drowning her on purpose.

"Have you spoken to Bobby yet? He was childhood best friends with Phillip and Kelsey. And what about his girlfriend, Michelle? She was also one of Josie's bridesmaids."

Suddenly a thought occurred to me. If Bobby was actually involved, Michelle might have more information than she had let on. What if Bobby and Michelle were working together all along? Hmm…I wondered what Michelle would have to gain by Phillip's death.

"I will be following up with Bobby today. He and his girlfriend stayed here at the resort last night. He's managed to evade me so far. When I spoke to him on the phone this morning, he claimed he wasn't emotionally stable enough to discuss the death of his friends. He also said he needed his attorney present before I tried to get him to say something incriminating."

He looked at his notebook again. "His girlfriend was also questioned with all the other guests who were in attendance. Was she with her boyfriend when you spoke to him?"

I shook my head. "I ran into her after everything happened with Phillip. She said she and Bobby had had a fight earlier in the day. She was obviously angry with him and made a comment about him sleeping it off." I paused. "Honestly, I was surprised that she didn't seem to have any compassion for her boyfriend, who'd lost his best friend."

Detective LeFleur made a note.

"Can I ask you one more question?" I said through my gritted teeth.

He pressed his lips together and nodded his head. I could see that I was getting on his nerves.

"Is Josie your main suspect?"

He frowned. "She's on the list. And now with Kelsey Clark's death, it adds a whole other layer to our investigation. We will continue questioning everyone who was connected to both her and Phillip Edwards."

Suddenly a brilliant idea popped into my head. "You can use me to try to get more information from them," I blurted out. "Obviously Kelsey was willing to talk to me."

Both the detective and Jack gave me funny looks.

"What I mean is, why not let me talk to Bobby and Michelle? He was really opening up to me yesterday, although he was drunk, but maybe he'll be more open to talking to me. I can go to them as a representative of the cruise line, which I am." I threw a side glance at Jack. "You can even put one of those hidden wires on me," I suggested. I didn't know what I was saying. Maybe the stress was starting to get the better of me. I probably needed to quit while I was ahead.

The detective smiled. "Ms. Walker, I appreciate your eagerness to help, but we are trained in these situations. This is what we do."

The detective's phone rang. He looked at it and stood up. "Excuse me for a minute."

As soon as he walked out of the room, I looked at Jack. "I totally think I could get more information from Bobby, Michelle, and Josie."

He frowned. "I'm sure you could, but we need to listen to the detective. They have a protocol to follow, and we shouldn't interfere, so you *need* to let them do their job."

Obviously I wasn't a detective, but I knew I could find out more, at least from Josie.

"You're probably right," I lied. I'd told Jack what he wanted to hear, for now, but I had every intention of getting my own answers.

CHAPTER ELEVEN

————

Detective LeFleur finally returned from his phone call and told us he had everything he needed from us. Luckily Jack wanted to discuss the press release with him, which gave me the opportunity to do my own investigating. I told the men I wanted to take a walk to clear my head, and they bought it. At least I think they did. Like my grandma used to say—"ask for forgiveness later."

My first task was to find Bobby and Michelle and talk to them. Their relationship seemed odd to me. Especially after Bobby had flirted with Chloe right in front of Michelle. Not to mention Michelle's remarks about Bobby after Phillip died. Maybe they had one of those open relationships, and I couldn't care less. It wasn't my place to judge, but I was curious about their friendship with Phillip and Josie.

I stopped at the concierge desk and flashed my very important Epic Cruise Line ID. That card had really come in handy over the last twenty-four hours. The sweet girl at the desk played right into my hands and without question gave me information on Bobby and Michelle's and Josie's rooms.

As the elevator climbed to the tenth floor, I rehearsed what I wanted to say to Bobby. I needed to be supportive, sympathetic, and careful with my words but still try to get as much information as I could. The doors opened, and I stepped out into the open hallway.

I moved slowly down the hall toward Bobby's room and stopped just before I reached it. That was when the doubts crept in. What was I doing? What if Bobby had murdered his two best friends? How stupid was I coming here alone to question him? I reviewed the different possibilities in my head and, despite my concerns, decided it was now or never.

I inhaled deeply and knocked on the door. My heart was pounding against the walls of my chest while I waited for someone to answer. After a few seconds, the door opened barely an inch. I could see through the crack that it wasn't Bobby. It was Michelle. I wondered if she'd forgiven him for his drunken state of the day before.

As soon as she saw it was me, she opened the door wider.

"Hi, Michelle. We met yesterday. I work for Epic Cruise Line." I pointed to my ID, which I'd conveniently clipped to my belt loop. I wasn't taking any chances.

"Oh, yes."

"Do you and Bobby have a minute to chat?"

Without answering, she stuck her head out of the door and looked up and down the hall.

"I'm by myself," I told her.

"Give me a second, okay?"

She closed the door, and I exhaled loudly. I assumed she was talking to Bobby, or maybe she was calling security on me? I considered making a run for it, but the door opened again a few seconds later.

"You can come in," she said, holding the door open for me.

I walked across the threshold. The room was the same layout as Kelsey's, with a grand seating room and the long hallway that led to a bedroom. The door to the bedroom was closed.

"Bobby will be right out. He's just getting changed."

Michelle sat down on a couch. She was wearing a short blue cotton dress and gold flip-flops. Her wavy auburn hair was pulled up into a high ponytail, and she wasn't wearing as much makeup as the day before.

"I'm glad you were able to work things out," I said cheerfully. "You mentioned you were upset with him yesterday."

She shrugged. "Yeah, it's a very difficult time for us right now. Certainly not the time for us to argue over silly little things."

My phone buzzed from my bag, which caused my stomach to do a flip. I prayed it wasn't Jack summoning me already. If it was my only shot to talk to Bobby, I had to take advantage of it. Thankfully, the text was from Chloe checking in. I didn't want Jack to know I was here yet.

I'd ignored Chloe's text and put my phone back in my bag just as the bedroom door opened. Bobby strolled out with a cup of coffee in his hand. His dark brown hair looked like it was still wet. He looked calm, relaxed, and sober in his jogging pants and T-shirt.

It struck me as odd that he looked so unfazed by the deaths of his friends, despite what he'd told Detective LeFleur. Was he really that unemotional? In the last twenty-four hours, I'd realized grieving was different for everyone, but at first glance he seemed completely unaffected.

I stood up to greet him. "Hi, Bobby. Thanks for agreeing to see me."

He waved his hand. "Sure. To what do we owe the pleasure?" He sat down next to Michelle and placed his hand on her leg. That was the first time I'd seen any real connection between the two of them.

I sat on the edge of the chair across from them. I hoped they didn't notice how uneasy I was feeling. I shouldn't be nervous because it was supposed to be a routine visit, not an interrogation. I gave them the same line I'd used with Kelsey about the cruise line wanting to make sure they were doing alright and asked them what we could do for them. "I know yesterday was a difficult day, and I can't imagine what you're going through after hearing about Kelsey."

Bobby took a sip of his coffee. "Yes, I don't think it's hit me yet. I feel like I've been in a complete daze since the detective broke the news," he answered. "It doesn't help that the police have been harassing me. They're relentless, even though I told them I won't talk without my attorney present. I know how this stuff goes. They'll twist my words and ask questions that might make me look bad. I had my issues with both Phillip and Kelsey—we've been friends since childhood and have had ups and downs. And there's no way I will go in there as a sitting duck."

I gave him a curious look. Why did he have such a big issue with talking to the police? *Did he have something to hide?*

"I know what you mean. I had to talk to them as well. Detective LeFleur informed us that Phillip's family is pushing hard for this investigation, which is completely understandable. Their son just died. I'm sure they're beside themselves."

Bobby pursed his lips. "I know why they want to question me, but I don't know anything. Regardless, I'm still not comfortable with them trying to put words in my mouth. I'll talk to them—with my lawyer present."

I wasn't sure if he was referring to Phillip's family or the police putting words into his mouth.

"Are you talking about the detective or Phillip's parents?" I asked casually. "I thought your families were super close?"

He nodded. "Yes, we're basically family. I was talking about the police—I know how this works. The pressure is on—they want to solve the case. I get it, but they're wasting their time with me when they should be looking elsewhere."

Hmm...elsewhere?

"Like where?" I asked as I lowered my voice.

He and Michelle exchanged glances.

"Well, his wife for starters!" he exclaimed.

Okay, now I was hopefully getting somewhere.

"Have you spoken to Josie?" I asked. "I was wondering how she's doing. She didn't come back to the ship last night."

He shrugged his shoulders. "I couldn't tell you. I have nothing to say to her either."

Michelle looked up from her phone and gave him a side glance. "Bobby, be nice."

He rolled his eyes. "I wasn't being mean. I just said I don't want to talk to her."

"I haven't seen her since yesterday," I told them. "The PR director of our company and I met with both her and Drew. It was hard because nothing I say will change what happened."

Bobby's face softened slightly. "Drew's a good man, a much better man than Phil. He was like a big brother to me. Phil never appreciated him, or anyone else for that matter."

Bobby was doing it again. Did he have anything good to say about Phillip?

"He seems very pleasant and slightly overwhelmed. He had a call from his father's lawyers while we were there."

Bobby shifted uncomfortably in his seat.

Hmm...there was definitely some legal history with these families that I needed to get information about. Why did he seem so worried when I mentioned the family lawyers?

"I imagine they have good representation," I added. "Do you know anything about their hotshot legal team?"

"How did Josie act?" he asked, avoiding my question about the lawyers. "I'm sure she put on a good show for you. She's very good about manipulating everyone around her. I almost fell for her act in the beginning—maybe I'm more gullible than I thought."

"Do you mind telling me more about Josie and Phillip?" I asked gently. "It's been such a long time since I've seen her. I don't know much about what life has been like for her since we were in fourth grade together."

Bobby leaned back on the couch and rubbed his forehead.

"I'm not trying to pry," I added. "I'm just trying to make sense of the whole situation I've gotten myself caught up in. I'm sure you can guess I have my own reasons for wanting answers. Don't forget, I was the person who pulled Phillip out of the hot tub, and as hard as I tried, I wasn't able to help him."

Bobby sat up and interlocked his fingers together. "I get it." He groaned. "Here's the short version: Phillip and I were best friends as kids, and our parents are still close. Kelsey was like a sister to us, and the three of us were inseparable for years." Bobby paused and cleared his throat, and for the first time I noticed the tiniest bit of emotion for his friends, or at least for Kelsey. "As we got older we drifted apart—it happens. A few years ago I had a venture idea for an online business, and I approached Phil about it because he'd always had a good eye and because everything he touched turned to gold. We brainstormed and came up with a plan. The idea became a reality practically overnight, as I'd expected. Unfortunately, Phil had a different plan on the side, and success was more important to him than his relationships. He basically took my idea and ran with it. He did cut me in financially but took all the credit for the initial idea. I hadn't protected myself because I didn't think I needed to, and he screwed me over. I was partying a lot at the time, so I didn't try to fight it. The only thing I cared about was collecting the paychecks."

"So what changed?" I asked. Did something else happen?"

Bobby stopped talking, and he looked like he was deep in thought. I tried to process the new information. Basically, Phillip had not only cheated on his wife, he'd also cut his best friend out of the business venture that was Bobby's idea. Phillip really was a piece of work.

"Things were starting to get back on track for us around the time he started dating Josie. We were talking again, and I thought we were finally moving on from our past issues." He paused. "She was okay at first, but then she started talking about marriage nonstop. I actually asked her why there was such a rush, given that they'd only dated a few months, and she gave me a story about Phillip being her soul mate and how much she couldn't wait to be a wife and mother. It was all very fairy tale-ish, and Phillip just went along with it. You remember that, Michelle?"

Michelle nodded, barely acknowledging our conversation. She seemed to be focused on her phone. I wondered if she was even listening to us.

"It was then that I started having doubts about her intentions. In the back of my mind, I was concerned about the company. I tried to warn Phillip, and his parents tried to warn him. Everyone in our inner circle didn't understand why they got married so quickly. Phillip and I were discussing my role in the company around the same time, so I was careful about how I addressed my concerns with him. Sure enough, before we knew it, they were planning their wedding. Now he's gone, and I'm not sure where that leaves me and my stake in the company."

"Are you sure Josie even wants the company?" I asked. "Maybe she really married Phillip for love and the rest doesn't matter to her."

Bobby stared at me like I had three heads. "That's funny," he said, even though he wasn't laughing. "I'm not surprised you would believe that. You and Josie are good friends."

I chewed my lip. "Well, we were friends when we were kids. I hadn't seen her in years until she and Phillip walked into my office on the ship."

"Then you really can't assume to know the type of person she is now," he snapped.

Ugh. This wasn't going the way I'd hoped.

"What about Kelsey?" I asked. "She seemed to have her own issues with Josie as well."

Michelle and Bobby looked at each other. "Kelsey has always been in love with Phillip ever since we were young. They had a short-lived fling, and Phillip moved on, but she didn't. I can't tell you how many times I told her to get on with her life. I think she really believed they would end up together."

"Kelsey was unstable," Michelle said flatly. "You could practically see her falling apart when Phil got married. I was surprised she didn't go ballistic at the wedding. She sat in the corner the entire night, drinking wine and staring off into space. It was weird."

"That's very sad," I said as I cleared my throat. "I heard the police are also investigating her death. I asked if they thought she committed suicide, but they don't think so."

Bobby pressed his lips together. He definitely seemed more emotional over Kelsey's death than Phillip's.

"Kelsey wouldn't do that," he insisted. "Despite what Phil did to her, she wasn't that far gone."

"Do *you* think Kelsey found out something about Phillip's death?" I asked. *Or did she follow through on her threat?* The thought gave me the chills. There was that old saying about a woman scorned, or something like that.

"Maybe she did. But the fact is that the only person who would benefit from Phillip's death is Josie," Bobby insisted. "Kelsey truly loved him, and he broke her heart."

"That's true," Michelle agreed.

I looked back and forth between the two of them.

"Did Josie know about their previous relationship?" I asked.

He rolled his eyes. "Probably, but I doubt that would have stopped her from marrying him. Money has a way of making you overlook certain things."

Michelle nodded.

"Are you saying that you believe Josie is behind all of this?" I asked. "I understand you didn't agree with their marriage, but do you really believe she's capable of such a terrible thing?"

Bobby rose to his feet. "I can't talk about this anymore. Thanks for coming by. I'm not sure if we'll be returning to the ship or not. I'm waiting on a call from my attorney, and then I'll know how to proceed. We might be staying here until it's time to head home."

I nodded. "I understand. I'm so sorry you weren't able to enjoy our ship."

Bobby walked toward the door, and I trailed behind him. "Can I ask you one more thing before I leave?"

I could sense he was tired of the questions by the way he abruptly ended the conversation, but it was my last chance.

"Fine."

"Why did you go on the cruise with Phillip and Josie if you didn't like her?"

Bobby frowned and looked at Michelle. "Would you like to answer that question?" he asked her. There was an irritated edge in his voice.

"I was in Josie's bride tribe," Michelle said. "Bobby is still mad about it."

I remembered seeing Josie with her friends at the pool yesterday. That seemed like a lifetime ago. It was crazy to think how much had changed in such a short period of time.

Michelle didn't seem to have as much animosity toward Josie as Bobby did.

"You aren't friends with her," he snapped. "You shouldn't have said yes."

"Are we really going to argue about this again?"

I stood awkwardly while they snapped at each other.

"She was marrying your childhood best friend. What was I supposed to say?"

Bobby shook his head. "Josie made a huge production of asking these women to be in her *bride tribe*. She sent them gifts and invited them to a fancy dinner."

Michelle was the one who'd agreed to go on the cruise with Phillip and Josie?

"So you came on the cruise because you were in the bridal party?" I asked.

"Thanks again for stopping by, Lexi," Bobby interrupted. Clearly he was done talking to me.

"Well, I appreciate your time. I hope everything gets resolved soon for all of you. And please reach out to us with any concerns. The cruise line will accommodate you in any way we can."

Bobby nodded before closing the door behind me.

I glanced at my phone. There was no word from Jack yet. I waited outside Bobby and Michelle's door for a few seconds while I tried to process everything I'd learned during my visit. One thing was for sure—it seemed like Bobby wanted me to believe that Josie was guilty.

CHAPTER TWELVE

———

My mind continued to race as I made my way to the eighth floor where Josie's room was located. I tried to wrap my head around my conversation with Bobby and Michelle. I wondered if I should quit while I was ahead. In a short amount of time, I felt completely intertwined in these people's lives. For some reason I'd had the brilliant notion to go rogue and do this on my own, when in reality I had no idea what I was doing. *Honestly, who did I think I was?*

Instead of giving in to my doubts, I knocked on Josie's door and waited. I wasn't as nervous about visiting her as I'd been about visiting with Bobby and Michelle. A few seconds later, she arrived at the door, and I gasped at her appearance. It wasn't the same Josie I'd reconnected with two days before, nor was it the new bride who pranced around the pool with her bride tribe hours before her husband was found floating in a fancy hot tub.

This woman looked disheveled—she wore no makeup, and dark gray shadows had appeared below her eyes, indicating she'd gotten little to no sleep. Her hair was a knotted mess, and she was wearing a pair of sweats that were too big for her small frame. *Maybe they were Phillip's?* I couldn't begin to imagine what she was going through, so who was I to judge her appearance?

"Hi, Josie." I hesitated as I tried to cover up my shock at seeing her in that state. She'd been much more put together when I spoke to her and Drew yesterday. Maybe everything was finally catching up to her, or maybe Kelsey's death had put her over the edge.

"Hey," she said. It was the first time she hadn't greeted me with her usual bubbly demeanor. She appeared sullen and her spirit completely broken.

"I hope I didn't wake you. I just wanted to see how you were doing." I stopped myself before making a comment about how she looked. I certainly didn't want to kick her while she was down.

She winced. "You didn't. I actually haven't slept at all."

"Are you sure you should be here?" she asked worriedly.

My stomach twisted and turned at her question because she was probably right. Most people would listen when authorities make a suggestion like that, but not me. I hoped I wasn't going to regret my decision.

"I don't plan to stay long, but how can I help you? The cruise line and I are still committed to assisting with anything you need, and you look like you're struggling, which is understandable."

She shook her head. "There's nothing you can do. That was nice that the cruise line sent my things over. Drew said he'd hold on to Phillip's things, but I wanted to keep them with me. These are Phillip's sweats."

I'd figured they were, judging by the way they hung loosely off her body.

"I assume you heard about Kelsey," she asked.

"Yes, I heard," I replied sadly. "I wish there was something I could say, but I can't find the words."

She rocked back on her heels as she peered behind me and down the hall. "You can come in really quick. I'd rather not discuss this in the hallway."

She grabbed my arm and pulled me into the room before I had a chance to object. We stood in the entryway, and she pulled her sleeves down to cover her hands. "I don't know what to do," she whispered. "Phillip's family, and probably everyone else, already thinks I drugged my husband, and now they're questioning me about Kelsey. His parents are using this against me, and it keeps getting worse. I can't sleep, I can't eat, I feel like I'm being watched, and I'm completely freaking out."

I pressed my lips together as I struggled with how to respond. The part about her being watched made me nervous. "I heard they found Kelsey's body in a hot tub, too," I said.

"I didn't do anything to Kelsey," she replied, an urgent tone in her voice. "Yes, I hated her, but that doesn't mean I killed her."

I was taken back by her admission.

"You hated her?" I asked. "I'm confused. I thought you were all good friends."

She rubbed her forehead. "Kelsey was Phillip's friend, not mine. She was on the same team as his parents with trying to convince him not to marry me. She wanted to destroy our happiness, and now—"

I watched her face twist with emotion, and I understood. It was hard to fathom everything that had happened.

Despite the tragic events—I also wondered if what Bobby and Kelsey had said was true. Was there another side to Josie I hadn't seen? Truthfully, it was one hundred percent possible. Sometimes it can take a while for people to show their true colors, certainly more than a day.

"Do you have any idea who would want Phillip and Kelsey dead?" I asked.

Josie frowned. "Probably Kelsey herself. She had loads of issues, and trust me, we'd be here all day if I tried to tell you about them. Long story short, she was obsessed with my husband, and he didn't feel the same way about her." She tightened her jaw. "Kelsey wanted me to suffer, and she's getting her wish. My entire life is hanging by a thread right now."

I thought about what Bobby and Michelle had said about Kelsey. And did Josie really know about her husband's relationship with Kelsey? Bobby made that comment about her only caring about Phillip's money, but I didn't believe it.

"Did something happen between Phillip and Kelsey?"

"What do you mean?" she asked with an edge in her voice. "I told you she was obsessed with him."

It didn't sound like Josie knew about Phillip and Kelsey's fling.

"Is there any way you can prove you didn't have anything to do with this? They have to have evidence to back their suspicions."

She sighed. "That's the problem," she said with panic in her voice. "I went to take a walk early this morning because I couldn't sleep. I thought the ocean air would help to clear my head a little." She paused and exhaled loudly. "While I was out, I ran into Kelsey, and we got into an argument. She must've been on something or drunk, because she started screaming at me. She was saying terrible things, told me I stole Phillip from her."

Josie stopped talking. Her face twisted as she tightened her jaw. I could see the pain she was in. I couldn't begin to imagine how she was feeling. I didn't say anything as I waited for her to collect her thoughts. She closed her eyes and exhaled again.

"First of all, Phillip was never hers, so how could I steal him? She's the one who wouldn't take a hint. She continued to push her way into our lives. I begged Phillip to ask her not to come here, but he wouldn't listen. He told me to just ignore her and, like it or not, she was family. I still don't understand why she wanted to come down here. We planned this trip with our closest friends who wanted to celebrate with us. She didn't support our marriage, so she shouldn't have been here."

I listened as I tried to put the pieces together.

"So you and Kelsey had an altercation this morning, and then she was found in the hot tub?"

Josie nodded. Her tired eyes were filled with worry.

Unfortunately, the events of the morning didn't bode well for Josie. I really wanted to tell her about the argument I'd overheard between Phillip and Kelsey, but it wasn't my place. I didn't want to cause this woman any more pain by revealing what they'd said. She was obviously experiencing enough of that already.

"I can't tell you how many times I tried to be nice to Kelsey because I knew their families were tight," she continued. "It's partly her fault his parents hated me so much. She did everything she could to try to sabotage me in front of them. Their parents had this ridiculous dream of their kids marrying each other, and then I came along and messed it up. The truth is,

I never had a chance with Andrew and Madeline. They were never going to accept me as part of their family."

I instantly remembered they were Phillip's parents.

I gave her a sympathetic look as I listened to every detail she told me. "Did you tell the police about your fight with Kelsey?" I asked. "It sounds like she was the aggressor."

She folded her arms tightly against her chest. "Someone already reported it before I had a chance to. A hotel staff member interrupted our argument, and that's when I left. I took a walk and came back here. A few hours later the detective showed up at my door with a million questions and told me Kelsey was dead."

She looked at the ceiling and sighed. "I wish they'd leave me alone. I need time to grieve my husband and come up with a plan. My whole life changed in an instant, and I have no idea what to do next."

It was hard not to stare at this person who was a shell of the woman she'd been the day before.

"I'm very sorry, Josie. I should leave you alone, too."

She held her hand out and touched my arm. "I wasn't talking about you, Lexi. You have no idea how much that means to have you here. I can't tell you how excited I was to see you again, and I'm so thankful that you're taking the time to listen to me. It makes me feel like I'm not alone." She bit her lip and looked away. "I wish I could go back and do things differently, maybe stand up for myself more."

My phone buzzed from my bag, making me jump. My heart sped up when I saw a message from Jack. I had to get back to him before someone came looking for me, if they weren't already. "My boss is texting me. I hope everything works out, Josie, and like I said, please reach out if you need anything else."

Just as I opened the door, I felt her hand on my shoulder. When I turned around, I was taken aback by Josie's blank stare.

"I think someone is trying to set me up, but I didn't do it, Lexi. You believe me, right?"

My phone buzzed again, causing panic to set in. I needed to get back to Jack as fast as I could. "I have to go," I told her. "Everything will work out, I'm sure of it."

I dashed out of her room and mentally prepared myself to tell Jack what I had done.

* * *

I probably looked very silly as I exited the elevator on the first floor and ran through the hotel on my way back to meet Jack. I tried not to look obvious, but a few people stared as I sped past them. I was breathing heavily when I burst into the meeting room.

Jack was sitting alone in one of the chairs, staring at his phone. He looked up at me and raised his eyebrows. "Why do you look so nervous, Lexi?"

Crap. I needed to work on being more subtle. I chuckled. "What do you mean? I'm not nervous."

The corner of his mouth curled up into a playful smile, which was both annoying and sexy. I guessed he'd already suspected I hadn't just come from taking a leisurely walk around the resort.

I grabbed one of the complimentary water bottles and took a sip. "Where's Detective LeFleur?"

Hopefully he wasn't out looking for me.

"On a conference call with Phillip's brother and their family lawyer." He paused and gave me a smug look. "By the way, Drew Edwards will probably be coming by to talk to us before we head back to the ship. Until then, why don't you tell me where you've been? I've been doing this long enough to know when a staff member is up to something."

Whether I liked it or not, he was my superior, so I needed to be honest with him. In my mind I tried to muster up every bit of confidence I had to tell him I had gone against the detective's advice.

"You're probably not going to like this, but I went to see Bobby and Josie," I said, sitting down in the chair closest to him.

He didn't look the least bit surprised. "As I figured. Didn't we just discuss letting the police handle the investigation? They are trained professionals who know how to deal with these situations, and you aren't."

I pushed my hair behind my shoulders. "Yes, but I think they're missing something."

Jack gave me a questioning look. "What? You think the detective doesn't know how to do his job?"

I ignored his comment and continued talking. "I think someone is setting Josie up and they aren't seeing it."

"Lexi, you don't know that for sure. Is that what Josie told you?"

I bit my lower lip. "Yes. But also because almost every question I've been asked comes back to Josie one way or another. My relationship with her, what other people said about her, what she said about other people—the list goes on."

"And you don't believe Josie Edwards had anything to do with the deaths of her husband or Kelsey Clark, do you?"

"No, I don't. But I actually have a few different theories."

Jack folded his arms against his chest, and I couldn't help but notice the way his dress shirt tightened around his biceps.

Gah! What is wrong with me?

"Alright, let's hear these theories you have, *Detective Walker.*"

I scowled. I wasn't sure if he was really interested in hearing my ideas or just humoring me. Either way, I wanted to tell him. I needed to talk to someone about it or I'd burst.

"Okay. I don't believe Josie had anything to do with it, but according to everyone, including Josie herself, many of Phillip's family and friends were against their marriage from the start. It sounds like Kelsey had a lot to do with that because of her own feelings for Phillip."

He leaned in toward me, close enough for me to catch a whiff of his cologne. The scent tickled my nose. It was clean and masculine.

I shifted around in my seat, trying to adjust my body so I wasn't distracted by his heavenly smell.

"So, you think Kelsey was involved with Phillip's death?"

I shrugged. "I think it's a definite possibility. Michelle and Bobby said she was in love with him and he strung her along. Kelsey was very angry at him for choosing Josie over her. I even heard her say she hoped karma would get him."

Jack gave a thoughtful look. "Okay, if that was the case, then what happened to Kelsey?"

I paused.

"Maybe she really did commit suicide. According to Michelle, she was completely unstable."

Jack shook his head. "The police don't think that's what happened. They have reason to believe there was a struggle. I'm sure they know what signs to look for."

I knew he was right, but that still didn't mean Josie did it.

"What if someone wanted Josie to take the fall for her death?" I asked. "I think Bobby could also be connected. He and Phillip had issues over the years. When the police questioned me about Phillip's death, they asked me about his business. Of course I knew nothing about it, but Bobby told me the company was his initial idea and Phillip took credit."

Jack opened his mouth to say something, but I continued talking.

"I think there's a chance Bobby's girlfriend Michelle could be in on it. Maybe there's something for her to gain from his death, perhaps financially or something related to the business? There's a weird vibe between the couple. She was really trying to make it sound like Kelsey had plenty of reason to want revenge on Phillip, and Bobby was visibly upset when she suggested it."

Jack shook his head. "I don't know. It seems like his wife is still the most likely suspect. Money, the company, and maybe revenge for him cheating on her? And as of now she was the last person who was with him, that we know for sure."

"That's exactly what I mean. Josie appears to be the most obvious, but is it too obvious? What if it was someone's intention to make it look like she *tried* to kill her husband, and it ended up going terribly wrong?"

I knew Jack was looking for holes in my theories, and there were a few.

"Alright, let's say this person didn't want him to die. How do you think Phillip got in the hot tub?" he asked. "Did they lure him there, or did he get in on his own, not knowing he was drugged? And what about Kelsey's death? Do you think someone wanted to frame Josie for that, too?"

I chewed on my lower lip while I thought.

Jack listened intently as I continued talking. "Kelsey was hysterical when she called me last night, and Josie told me they got into a heated argument this morning. It must've been bad because a hotel staff member had to break it up. Maybe she was so distraught over Phillip's death that she snapped. The fact that their bodies were both in hot tubs is eerie."

He rubbed his forehead. "I have to agree with you about that."

Jack grew quiet while I sipped my water.

I needed to explain why I was so committed to finding out what really happened. I wanted this to end so I could return to my life and career I loved. "I know you think I should stay out of it, but please put yourself in my shoes for a minute. My shift two nights ago began by reconnecting with a dear childhood friend. I helped them schedule two days of port fun, as I had with many other guests. Josie and Phillip were supposed to return to the ship to finish the sailing on board with us. While in port I had planned to come here to make sure our guests were receiving the best service possible. I stopped by the Edwards' party with your permission and was put in a situation to use my lifeguard training." I paused to catch my breath. "Unfortunately, my efforts weren't enough. As long as there's an investigation going on and I'm wrapped up in it, I'm going to do my part to find out the truth. I'm extremely worried that I could be affected by the outcome if Josie is somehow found guilty. We have a history, and I was with her prior to finding Phillip. I know you only care about Epic Cruise Line's reputation, and so do I, but I need to advocate for myself, too."

My lower lip began to shake as I finished my explanation. I closed my eyes in an effort to hold back my tears. However, I failed miserably. I buried my face in my hands. I'd tried so hard to prove to Jack that I was holding it together, but it had become too much. These deaths had affected me. I'd just had a conversation with Kelsey the night before, and even though I didn't know Phillip was drugged, I attempted to save his life.

As I tried to pull myself together, I felt two arms wrap around me. I didn't uncover my eyes, but I knew it was Jack by his scent. I abandoned all worries about him being my boss's boss's boss or trying to keep it together. I was emotional, and he was comforting me—that was it. I didn't read too much into his gesture, either. He let me cry into his shirt while I rested my cheek on his chest. A few seconds later I pulled away and dabbed the corners of my eyes with one of the hotel's signature cocktail napkins.

"I'm sorry," I said through my sniffles.

He gave me a sympathetic nod. "Don't be. My mum says a good cry is necessary to get those emotions out."

I lowered my head. "I agree with your mum—er mom, although it's not professional behavior."

"Yes, well, this isn't a typical day on the job," he reminded me.

No, it wasn't. Thank goodness.

"Let's be honest. I'm sure this isn't your first emotional breakdown. After all, you are a Miami Dolphins fan."

I rolled my eyes but let a giggle escape. I appreciated his attempt to cheer me up. "Thank you. I needed to laugh."

It was nice of him to be patient and allow me to break down for a few minutes. Like his *mum* said, that cry was what I needed, and I was already feeling a little better.

"Fantastic. Now that you've had a good cry, we need to sit down and figure out how to address other unforeseen twists that may come up. I've already issued a statement to the press on behalf of the cruise line. Now we wait to see what else the authorities need from us. They know we're sailing out tomorrow night, so our time here on the island is limited."

I never thought I'd say it, but the idea of leaving paradise sounded wonderful. Hopefully I had somewhere to go when all was said and done. "I'm ready to do whatever I have to, but I need your help with something."

He eyed me suspiciously. "What's that?"

"Let me continue my search for what really happened."

"Lexi—"

"You have to admit I'm on to something here," I interrupted before he could shoot me down.

He folded his arms. "I do believe you're on to something, but I still feel you need to stay out of it now. You've done all you can to help. The more involved you become from this point on, the more Epic Cruise Line *and you* are in the line of fire. There are just too many things that could go wrong. Not to mention if someone is desperately trying to cover up the truth, they aren't going to like your continued involvement."

"Jack—" I interrupted.

"I'm sorry, but you must let Detective LeFleur and his team do their job. Your interference is just going to complicate this situation even more. The last thing we need is for you to be accused of tampering or poking around while the authorities are trying to gather evidence and get resolution. You did your part by trying to rescue Phillip. It's out of your hands now."

It was obvious he wasn't going to change his mind, but that wasn't going to stop me. I needed to protect myself, and I had every intention of being careful. The last thing I wanted to do was put a target on my own back. I just hoped I didn't already have one.

CHAPTER THIRTEEN

———

The clock was ticking, and as far as I was concerned Jack didn't need to know that I wasn't giving up on my quest to find out the truth. After I'd admitted to him that I'd been off doing my own investigating, we were waiting for Drew to stop by. His pending visit actually fit into my plan perfectly. Although Drew wasn't a guest on the ship, the cruise line maintained they would assist his family with any needs following his brother's death, and Jack wanted to reiterate it.

I stayed in the meeting room while Jack took a call and waited for Drew to come. When I pulled my phone out of my bag, I noticed two missed calls from Chloe. Knowing her, she was dying for an update and probably worried about me after I'd left the ship in such a hurry.

"Finally. Is everything alright?" she answered in lieu of a greeting.

"Hello to you, too."

"Yes, hello. I've been waiting by the phone for you to call me back. I just told Levi that you ran off to the resort with Jack Carson."

"Chloe, please don't start any crazy rumors. That's the last thing I need right now." It was probably too late to be worried about gossip. I was sure the rest of the staff and crew were already talking.

"I didn't start any rumors. Everyone just wants to make sure you're alright."

"Today has definitely been interesting. I had some informative conversations with Josie, Bobby, and Michelle. Jack told me to stop interfering in the investigation, and I know the detective won't be happy when he finds out. But before that I kind of had a meltdown in front of Jack."

"You didn't."

"I sure did."

"How did he react?"

I told her how Jack had been sincere and supportive during my emotional outburst.

"So Jack was comforting you? That was very sweet of him."

Typical Chloe. I knew the wheels in her head were already turning. "Don't overreact. He was only comforting me because I was doing the ugly cry. Everyone knows most men get uncomfortable when a woman has tears pouring down her cheeks."

"Mmhmm."

"What was he supposed to do? Sit like a statue and show no compassion? Don't make it into more than it is."

"Lexi, he could've given you a tissue and told you not to worry. Comforting you with a hug is certainly more intimate. Perhaps he isn't as uptight as you thought."

I rolled my eyes. "He was just being a decent human being because I was a mess. And I'm sure he doesn't want me falling apart while the cruise line is already getting so much attention."

It didn't matter what I said. I knew Chloe already had her mind set on something romantic coming out of this intensely traumatic experience. Here I was, worried about whether I'd still have a job, and she was more concerned about my personal life. She was a good friend but a hopeless romantic to the core. She probably imagined Jack riding in on his white horse and saving the damsel in distress (me).

"Anyway, he told me to let the detective do his job. Unfortunately, I've come too far to just give up now. What Jack Carson doesn't know won't hurt him."

"Are you sure about this, Lexi? Maybe you should listen to him."

I explained my newest theories after talking to Bobby, Michelle, and Josie. "Based on what I've heard, Phillip made quite a mess for himself. Of course that doesn't mean he deserved what happened to him, but if Josie didn't drug him, she shouldn't take the blame for it. And I was only doing what I had been trained to do. I had to act in case the Edwards did accuse me of conspiring with Josie. It sounds like they hate her that much."

The door of the meeting room opened, and Jack walked in.

"Chloe, I've got to go. I'll see you tonight," I said. I ended the call before she could say good-bye.

"Drew Edwards should be here in a few minutes." Jack sat down and started typing on his phone.

Neither of us said anything as we waited. The silence was awkward, and I felt like I needed to make conversation. "Thank you for being so understanding about my behavior earlier." I cleared my throat. "Outbursts are very unusual for me. I'm normally very calm and let things roll off my back." I wanted to remind him that I was good under pressure. There was nothing worse than a lifeguard who fell apart when faced with a stressful situation.

"Lexi, I know this hasn't been easy on you."

I shook my head. "No, it hasn't. I'm worried—about my reputation, my job, and—"

Our conversation was interrupted by a knock on the door followed by Drew Edwards popping his head into the room.

Jack stood up and went to greet him at the door.

Drew gave me a slight wave. He sat down next to Jack and rubbed his hands on his pant legs.

I noticed his resemblance to Phillip a bit more today. He was taller and thinner, but they had the same square jawline and brown eyes. Drew's warm demeanor hadn't changed, even with all the worry, stress, and chaos.

"Thanks for coming. Like I said on the phone, Epic Cruise Line wants to help your family in any way we can. I know it isn't much, but we've already issued a refund for all cruise expenses to Josie, as well as to Bobby and his guest."

"That's very kind of you," Drew said.

I guessed Drew didn't care about the thousands of dollars they'd paid for the cruise and all expenses that went with it. It was common knowledge that the Edwards family wasn't struggling for money.

"I'm sorry to hear about Kelsey," I added.

"Thank you," he said, dropping his head. He closed his eyes and inhaled deeply. "The Clarks are part of our family, and losing her is almost like losing Phillip. As you can imagine, everyone is in complete shock right now. Their deaths have devasted our parents."

"Have you spoken to Josie?" I asked. Out of the corner of my eye, I glanced at Jack. I was probably walking a fine line, but I was just trying to be proactive.

Drew pressed his lips together. "Yes. I've been trying to help her, but my parents are giving me a lot of grief about it. Dealing with the police, the lawyers, and Josie has been overwhelming. I should be mourning my brother, but I can't begin to do that because I'm dealing with this investigation."

"Are your parents coming down here?" Jack asked.

He shook his head. "They want to, but I'm trying to get them to hold off. There's nothing they can do now. They haven't released Phillip's body yet. Of course my mother is already trying to make plans for the memorial, but there's too much up in the air right now to think about a service."

Wow, I hadn't even thought about funeral services. If it was difficult for me to think about, it must've been unbearable for the family.

"I'm not looking forward to it," he said sadly. "There's a lot of animosity between Josie and my parents, so planning any kind of service will be difficult. I'm really trying my best to stay neutral. I wish I could get my parents to lighten up a little, because whether they like it or not, Josie was Phillip's wife."

Drew's face twisted. "The truth is, my brother had a lot of strained relationships—skeletons in his closet. He did things that hurt the people in his life. I thought everything was getting better and that he was mending tattered relationships, but I was wrong." He paused. "And Kelsey's death is completely shocking. I don't know what to think."

Drew was confirming what I was thinking. One of Phillip's actions most likely led to his demise. I just wasn't sure which action it was.

"I hope I'm not crossing the line by asking you this, but I heard there were some issues between Kelsey and Phillip. Do you think they are related?"

Jack's eyes grew wide. I was definitely crossing the line.

"Kelsey was head over heels in love with my brother from the time she could walk. She tried to come between every relationship he had, and for the most part she succeeded. I told Phillip he needed to straighten things out with her, but he ignored it and let it build up. I knew it would eventually come to a head."

"I'm very sorry that you're all going through this. Such a terrible tragedy," Jack said sincerely.

Drew put his hand out to me. "Lexi, I just wanted to reiterate what I told you yesterday. I watched you try to save my brother. Thank you for your efforts."

I gave him a weak smile. I wished his words calmed my nerves, but they didn't.

"Thank you for saying that," I said. "I wish I could have done more to help. I hope your parents know that too."

"Lexi is worried because of her past friendship with Josie," Jack added.

Drew gave me a curious look.

"After hearing about Josie's issues with your parents, I was wondering how they would feel about our friendship. And I was with her when we found Phillip..." I trailed off.

Drew shook his head. "I'm not sure what you've heard about my parents, but they aren't terrible people. Right now they're angry, grief-stricken—but they aren't malicious."

I tried to have sympathy for his parents and reminded myself that I couldn't rely solely on Josie's opinion about them. She had reasons to feel the way she did, but I knew there were always two sides to every story.

"Of course they aren't," Jack agreed. "I can't fathom the pain they're experiencing right now. We aren't trying to make assumptions or upset you. We appreciate your willingness to talk to us."

"Unfortunately, there's not much more I can do at this point," Drew said. "Until the investigation is complete, we won't know what really happened to my brother. I have my own suspicions, and I've shared those with the police."

"What do you think really happened?" I asked curiously.

"Lexi," Jack said. He gave me a stern look.

"It's fine," Drew said. "Of course these are just theories, but Bobby and my brother were at odds all the time. They've had an ongoing feud for as long as I can remember, but out of respect for our parents, they kept it from escalating any further. Out of the blue, Bobby's new girlfriend Michelle and Josie became friends, and before we knew it, the four of them ended up going on the cruise together. Josie can be somewhat naïve and really believed Michelle was her friend."

"So, Michelle is pretending to be Josie's friend?" I asked. "Why?"

Drew shrugged. "I'm not sure exactly." He paused and let out a deep sigh. "Anyway, my brother and Bobby had some issues with business dealings."

"Josie told me that he and Bobby were best friends. I never would've guessed they were ever at odds by the way she described their friendship."

"Oh, it wasn't just Bobby. Phillip and Kelsey also had their problems, and as much as I loved her like a sister, I think my brother drove her to the brink—" Drew hung his head. "The fact is, my brother and a very dear friend are dead, and now we have to try to move on without them."

It seemed more and more likely to me that Bobby and Michelle could be involved in these deaths, but it felt like something was still missing. I couldn't put my finger on what it was, though. I remained quiet while Jack thanked him for talking to us. Drew said he'd keep us posted on any new developments, and Jack said the same.

I didn't say anything after Drew left. It was a lot to process, and I was growing more exhausted by the second. Ultimately, it was a sad situation for everyone involved. These people were all a family at one time, and the possibility that they could hurt one of their own was tragic.

"You haven't said much," Jack said finally. "What are you thinking about?"

I sighed. "I don't know. I feel like Bobby and Michelle are deeply involved in this, but something still isn't adding up."

Jack leaned his head pensively to the side. "I know you want answers for your own peace of mind, but it's out of your hands."

I nodded. "I know."

Jack stretched back in his chair and put his hands behind his head. "Try not to worry about it and let the detective do his job."

"I'm just wondering if it was all planned out. Was coming on this trip some twisted way of seeking revenge on Phillip? I know the guy did some rotten things, but for someone to take another person's life… Are people really capable of this kind of stuff?"

"Unfortunately, yes," he said.

Ugh. That was a hard pill to swallow. I'd seen movies and heard stories, but realizing it could've happened here was unbelievable.

"Lexi, you're going to drive yourself mad. You need to let it go."

I understood what he was saying. The only problem was, I was invested now. It wasn't just about me anymore. It was about this family and my friend Josie.

CHAPTER FOURTEEN

———

I stretched out and put my feet up on the chair across from me. Jack left to fetch us some lunch, so I used those few minutes to jot down some notes from my conversations with Bobby, Michelle, Josie, and Drew.

Maybe I could become a private investigator if my career with Epic Cruise Line didn't work out. I loved working on the ships and wasn't ready to leave yet, but the future was definitely on my mind. Realistically, I had to weigh my options if this ended badly and I lost my job. I felt like Jack and I were coming to an understanding, but I didn't know where I stood with lifeguarding.

I thought about what it'd be like to not be on the ship anymore and about my parents. I usually emailed an update to them once a week. In my two years with the cruise line, the most dramatic thing I'd ever told them was about staying out of the paths of hurricanes. They were in for quite a story next week. I didn't want to stress them out until I had more information, but they needed to know what happened with Phillip. My mother always worried about me being a lifeguard and even questioned whether I had PTSD from my experience of almost drowning in the ocean. I hated that I had to tell them we'd lost a guest, despite the fact that it wasn't my fault.

I put the pen down and pushed my notes away. My head was throbbing, probably caused by lack of restful sleep and all the stress that'd been building over the last twenty-four hours. I rested my chin on my hands and closed my eyes. I was ready to give in to my exhaustion when Jack returned with a bag full of food. He looked even more relaxed than he had earlier. His sleeves were rolled up, and his shirt had a few wrinkles in it.

He narrowed his eyes when he noticed my head on the table. "What's the matter? Did I miss something?"

I shook my head. "No, I just have a headache."

"You're probably hungry. I'm famished," he said. "Why don't we eat outside and get some fresh air?"

That sounded nice. I grabbed my phone and followed him out toward a covered terrace that overlooked the resort. The clear blue ocean water was the perfect backdrop. The tall palm trees were swaying with the light breeze coming off the sea, and the white sand sparkled under the midday sun. I soaked up the view for a few seconds. The familiar scent of the ocean was invigorating. Jack had been right about getting some fresh air. I really needed it.

I sat down as Jack unloaded the food onto the table. I watched as the items kept coming—it was like Mary Poppins' bottomless carpet bag. There were so many options: a ham and cheese croissant, a turkey and avocado wrap, a tuna salad sandwich, hummus and vegetables, a chef salad, a Caesar salad, fresh fruit, potato chips, and cookies.

"Did you invite everyone in the hotel to join us for lunch?" I asked with a giggle.

He gave me a sheepish smile. "I wasn't sure what to get, and it all looked good, so I bought every option they had in the market. Take whatever you want."

Normally I'd choose the most nutritious option, especially in front of a man who looked like Jack, but not today. I reached for the croissant and a bag of chips. I couldn't care less about eating healthy. It was all about comfort food at that point, so I grabbed two large chocolate chip cookies as well. As I unwrapped the croissant, it occurred to me that I'd barely eaten anything yesterday. No wonder my head was pounding.

I was about to take a bite when Jack started talking. "Tell me more about yourself, Lexi."

I gave him a curious look. We hadn't discussed our personal lives at all other than our choices in football teams, and considering we'd been in nonstop crisis mode since we met, I didn't think it was important or that he cared. Regardless, I welcomed a conversation that didn't revolve around death, hot tubs, potential lawsuits, or scandals.

"Oh, well, I'm originally from Winter Park, Florida as you know. I went to college at the University of Central Florida, majored in business, but I was bored with it. I hated business so much, and I was miserable and confused about what I wanted to do next. I'd worked as a lifeguard part-time since high school and thought it'd be fun to work on a cruise ship. Two years later, here I am."

He beamed.

I recalled our conversation about football teams when he mentioned he'd lived all over the world. "I'm sure it's not as exciting as living in many different countries, though," I added.

"What're you talking about? You've been traveling for two years now."

I smiled. "That's true, and I've loved every second of it." It didn't hurt to remind him how much I enjoyed my career.

"Which port city is your favorite?" he asked.

At first I was confused about all the questions, but I realized he was trying to distract me from the investigation, and for that I was grateful.

"Wow, that's a hard one," I said. "How about you?"

He took a sip of water and gave a thoughtful look. "Ah, I'd probably say Norway or the Amalfi Coast. I love Venice, too."

It was refreshing to have a normal conversation. "I haven't done the Norway itinerary yet. Hopefully in the future." I took every advantage to drop a hint about my future employment with the cruise line.

"Have you worked on every ship in our fleet?" I asked. Since he'd showed so much interest in my career, I figured I should inquire about his, as well. And I was curious to learn more about Jack.

"Almost. I started my career in Guest Relations four years ago and worked my way up. It's been a fantastic experience."

"Until now?"

He shrugged. "What happened on this sailing is unfortunate, but I'm not unrealistic. Bad things are bound to happen. We transport thousands of passengers three hundred and sixty-five days a year."

I'd never thought of it that way. The situation with Phillip's death was unique, but sadly it wasn't completely impossible. Maybe not the details of his death, but it was certainly likely that a guest could drown in a hot tub at any given time.

"Well, it will be nice to move on to our next group of passengers and start over."

He nodded. "I have to agree with you on that."

Obviously Jack was already moving on. However, I wasn't ready to give up yet, and the minutes were ticking. If I wanted to find out what really happened, I had to move quickly. The question was how? I'd already had conversations with everyone who was close to the situation.

"You should feel proud, Lexi. I don't think I've worked with anyone who cared about our guests this much. If everyone at Epic Cruise Line showed this much dedication, we'd be unstoppable."

I felt my cheeks get hot. Even if I was unable to find out the truth, maybe I'd proven myself as an asset to the company. Perhaps something good could still come out of the tragedy.

After lunch we returned to the meeting room, where Detective LeFleur was waiting.

"Mr. Carson, Ms. Walker, we appreciate your willingness to come out here again."

"Were you able to find out anything else about the deaths?" I asked.

He pressed his lips together. "We gathered as much information as we could."

"Great. We'll be heading back soon, then," Jack said.

"Another thing. Bobby Perry and his girlfriend will not be returning to the ship. They want to make arrangements for the remainder of their things to be brought here."

I glanced at Jack.

"Absolutely. I'll get that taken care of when we return to the ship," Jack said.

That was interesting. Bobby told me he wasn't sure if they were staying or finishing the vacation on the ship. Did that mean Bobby and Michelle were moving up the suspect list?

"Is that normal protocol?" I asked. "Do they have to stay in port because of their connection to the victims?"

Jack threw another stern glance at me.

The detective forced a smile. "It depends on the case."

Detective LeFleur abruptly excused himself before I had a chance to ask him anything else. Clearly he didn't want to continue our conversation. Suddenly I realized what I needed to do.

"We need to pack up Bobby and Michelle's things," I blurted out.

Jack looked up at me. "What?"

"Think about it. What if there's something in their room on the ship that would link them to Phillip's or Kelsey's murder? Maybe something about the business or why they came on the cruise."

Jack gave me a skeptical look. "I doubt they'd leave anything to incriminate themselves."

I knew he was going to say that. Now I had to think of something to convince Jack to let me into their room. I didn't want to leave the Bahamas without knowing the truth.

"Okay, what if I made a deal with you?" I said. "Let me pack their bags. After that I promise I'll bow out and let the police handle it."

He raised his eyebrows. "You probably should've bowed out already."

I opened my mouth to argue but quickly closed it. Jack wasn't going to change his mind, but that didn't mean I was done. I just had to find a way to search their stateroom on my own before it was packed up.

"I know you want to help, but I feel good after talking to Drew," Jack added. "Let's not do anything else that could jeopardize the investigation."

I nodded. Regardless, I felt exhilarated and nervous about what would happen next. One thing was for sure. In my heart I didn't believe Josie was guilty, and I was going to do everything I could to help prove it. I had twenty-four hours to do what seemed impossible, but I was ready.

CHAPTER FIFTEEN

———

It felt so good to be back on board our beautiful ship. Despite being only a few miles away from the Paradise Island Resort, it felt comfortable and safe. As soon as we returned, Jack excused himself to his office. I had to hurry if I was going to check out Bobby and Michelle's stateroom.

On my way to change, I stopped by the Grande Piano Bar to see Chloe.

Tracey was just leaving when I arrived. She was another one of our ship's performers.

"Lexi, you're back," she said, sounding surprised. She was wearing an oversized white sweatshirt and yoga pants. "Everyone has been so worried. How are you?"

I smiled. "I'm alright. Thanks for asking."

She nodded slowly. Obviously she didn't know what else to say, and I couldn't blame her. I'd been expecting that kind of response when I'd returned to the ship.

"I'm late for rehearsal, but I'm glad you're okay."

I watched as she hurried off before I made my way into the piano bar.

As I expected, Chloe was on stage rehearsing for her sets and stopped mid-chorus as soon as she saw me.

"Lexi, what a relief," she called. "Come up here."

She played a daunting tune on the piano as I made my way toward the front of the bar.

"Very funny. Is that the tune from *Jaws*?"

She laughed as I sat next to her on the piano bench and ran my fingers over the keys. I didn't have a musical bone in my body, so it sounded more like a toddler was banging on the keyboard than actual music.

"You must be exhausted. Did anything else happen at the resort? And please don't say another person ended up in a hot tub."

I laughed nervously. It wasn't funny, but nothing would have surprised me anymore. "No, thankfully not," I replied. "It just feels like this will never end. I thought yesterday was a long day, but today is beginning to feel like it's even longer."

"Poor you. Did you find out any more information?"

I gave Chloe the condensed version of my day since I'd last spoken to her. "I know Jack wants me to stay out of it, but I feel in my gut that I need to help. I even asked him if I could pack up Bobby and Michelle's things, and he was dead set against it. I feel like that might be our last chance at finding something that links them to Phillip's death."

I pushed my hair behind my ears. "I know Jack doesn't understand why I'm still so invested."

Chloe tapped a few keys. "He has a point. Lexi, you're going to have to leave it alone and let things fall where they may."

I sighed. "I will—as soon as I feel like I've done everything I can."

She frowned. "I think you're putting way too much pressure on yourself."

She was probably right, but I wasn't ready to give up yet.

I shrugged. "Anyway, Jack doesn't think we'll find anything in Bobby's room."

She made a face. "I'm afraid I agree. Do you really think he'd be stupid enough to leave something out that could be used against him? Did the police even check his room on the ship?"

I shrugged. "I don't know. Probably. But isn't it possible that they could've missed something? It happens on TV all the time."

"I suppose it is, but what makes you believe you'll find anything?"

I shrugged. "Maybe I won't, but at least I'll know I tried."

Suddenly Josie's distraught expression from earlier that morning flashed through my mind. "Chloe, you would've been shocked if you had seen Josie today. I felt so sorry for her."

"I'm sure," Chloe exclaimed. "Could you imagine coming on a vacation and watching your new husband die right in front of your eyes? The woman will need loads of therapy. Whether she's innocent or guilty, I don't know how someone could live with themselves after going through something so terrible."

"That's why I'm searching for answers. My gut is still telling me she's innocent even after everything I've seen and heard about her. The problem is, I don't know how to prove it, and after seeing Josie today, I don't think she has any fight left in her. That's why I have to at least try to go to Bobby and Michelle's stateroom."

Chloe stood up from the piano and picked up her water bottle. "Let's go, then. I'll help you search their room."

She was already walking toward the door when I ran to catch up to her. "Not so fast. I don't want to drag you into this. I need to do this alone."

She folded her arms. "Too bad. I'm going with you. You need emotional support after your ordeal."

I giggled. "Nice try, but I'm already on thin ice. If Jack finds out, I don't know what he'll do." I appreciated her for wanting to support me. Although I'm sure the idea of snooping for clues excited her, too.

"What exactly are you hoping to find?" she asked.

I shrugged. "Anything that might connect them to these deaths. Even the tiniest clue might help Josie. I'm out of options, and we're sailing out tomorrow. The countdown is on, and if I don't find anything, then it may be a lost cause."

I thought about what could be hiding in Bobby's room. I certainly didn't expect to find a descriptive plan on how to drug and kill a friend, but maybe there'd be something that would raise a red flag or two, something the authorities might have missed.

"So how was the rest of the day with Jack?" Chloe asked with a mischievous gleam in her eye.

I shook my head. It was not the time to talk about Jack and me spending time together.

"Don't you have to get back to work?"

She glanced at the time. "I'm meeting up with DJ Suz in a little while. She asked me to help out in the Broadway Lounge tonight after my set. There's a great group of passengers on this sailing."

"That sounds fun."

Hearing Chloe talk about the evening's events reminded me that life was still carrying on outside of Phillip's and Kelsey's sudden deaths. I'd missed out on mingling and meeting other guests on the ship because I'd been so wrapped up with Josie and their situation.

"So when should I meet you to pay a visit to Bobby and Michelle's room?"

I sighed. "Chloe."

She held up her hand. "Enough. I'm going with you whether you like it or not."

I knew better than to try to talk her out of it, so I agreed to meet her twenty minutes later. Now we just had to get inside, and luckily we had quite a few friends on the ship who could help us out.

"I'll take care of getting us in the room," Chloe insisted. "My friend in Guest Relations owes me big."

"Are you sure you want to get mixed up in this?" I asked. "Jack made it very clear that he's against any further involvement from me or anyone else from Epic Cruise Line."

Chloe gave me a wicked smile. "I never back down from a challenge."

That was true, and I had no doubt she would succeed in her quest.

After leaving the bar, I stopped by the Port Adventures offices. I hadn't been there since the night I met with Phillip and Josie. Thankfully it was quiet, because I wasn't in the mood to answer any questions yet. Our department usually closed during the day while in port. Besides me, there were two other staff members, Caleb and Trina, who worked in the department, and both of them were new to Epic Cruise Line. I was sure there were plenty of stories being told about me behind the scenes, and I wasn't looking forward to dealing with the fallout after this was all over.

I sat in my chair and swiveled from side to side. The silence was deafening. After a few minutes, I logged into my computer and pulled up Phillip and Josie's reservation. I didn't know what I was looking for, but I clicked on the Port Adventures tab. My heart sank when I saw the *Paradise Island Resort Concierge Day* and *Ultimate Sting Ray Experience* listed on their profile. I returned to their main profile page, and something caught my eye.

Although my vision was almost perfect, I leaned in to get a better look at my computer screen. Under emergency contacts, Kelsey's name was the first one listed for Phillip and Josie, followed by Phillip's parents. Wow, it seemed crazy to me that Kelsey of all people was listed as an emergency contact for Josie. Poor Josie. It seemed like she was on her own in Phillip's world. However, I guess that's what she chose when she married him. She'd briefly mentioned her mother and how sick she'd been, but from what I'd gathered, everyone else who came to the Bahamas was a friend or relation to Phillip.

Phillip must've made the travel arrangements, but why would he have listed Kelsey first, knowing how she felt about Josie?

I stared at the computer screen for a few seconds before I got another idea. I typed Bobby's name in the search box. His and Michelle's reservations popped up, and I quickly scanned through it. His parents were listed as emergency contacts on his file, and there was no mention of Kelsey. Nothing else about his profile seemed off to me.

I looked up to make sure my office door was still closed. Technically, I had entered forbidden territory by searching their profiles, but I didn't care anymore. Time was fleeing, and I had to get more information.

I glanced at the clock on my computer screen—it was almost time to meet up with Chloe. I logged out of my computer and moved quickly through the ship, greeting guests along the way. When I returned to my room, I changed into a blue blouse with bell sleeves and black pants. I reattached my name badge and brushed my teeth.

My heart began to race at the thought of possibly finding something in Bobby and Michelle's room. I just hoped my efforts would somehow pay off. All joking aside, maybe I'd make a good detective after all.

CHAPTER SIXTEEN

———

My heart was beating rapidly inside my chest. Jack would be furious if he found us searching through Bobby and Michelle's things. Chloe had asked her friend Chantelle from Guest Relations to let us in and to keep watch, but we still had to move quickly. Our ship had a few different styles of cabins, and as expected, Bobby and Michelle had a balcony suite on a higher deck. They obviously intended to take full advantage of Phillip and Josie's generosity. One thing was for sure, even if they weren't involved in Phillip's death, they were still crappy friends.

"Look at all of this stuff. Can you believe those two?" I asked, pointing to unopened bottles of champagne and gourmet chocolates. They must've ordered these items to enjoy upon returning to the ship. "They were totally using Phillip and Josie, ordering bottle service and taking full advantage of their generosity. Bobby can't stand Josie, and based on what he told me, he didn't care for Phillip either."

"Are you surprised?" Chloe asked as she continued opening and closing drawers. "Wow, Michelle really has impeccable taste," she added. Chloe had already tried on a pair of gorgeous gold wedges and was now sifting through a large suitcase.

Unfortunately, I hadn't found anything unusual yet. I wondered what Bobby and Michelle had taken to the resort. I remembered seeing a few smaller bags when I went to their room to talk to them. They must've taken extra clothes to change into following the party yesterday.

While Chloe looked through the bag, I noticed something sticking out of a side pocket. I reached over and pulled out an ivory envelope with a note card inside. I read it to myself.

Dear Michelle,

I'm so grateful that you will be beside me on the happiest day of my life. Can you believe we did it? Seeing Phillip and Bobby together is the best present we could ask for. Let's keep it that way. We can't wait to celebrate with you in the islands.

I wanted to give you a little something extra to remind you how much we appreciate your friendship.

Much love, Josie

"Look at this," I said. I handed Chloe the note and waited silently as she read it.

"No wonder Michelle wanted to be in Josie's bride tribe," she exclaimed. "Who wouldn't want to be showered with gifts and vacations?"

"Does that sound like a woman who wanted her husband dead or like someone who's excited about starting her new life with her husband?"

"You really believe she's innocent, don't you?" Chloe asked.

I sat down on the bed and looked around the stateroom. "Yes. I do. And I think Bobby, Michelle, and Kelsey all had a hand in Phillip's death."

"Then how did Kelsey die?" Chloe asked.

I paused as I recalled the last conversation I had with her.

"Kelsey was hysterical when she called me," I said. "As angry as she was with Phillip, it seemed like she regretted the things she said during their last conversation. She hated Josie for taking him away from her. She did say he was murdered, just not by who. Maybe she was going to come clean to the police and someone stopped her. Don't you think it's possible?"

Chloe chewed her bottom lip. "I suppose it is."

I checked the front compartment of the suitcase and pulled out a yellow folder.

I opened it and glanced at its contents.

"Whoa!" Chloe exclaimed. "What are those?"

I raised my eyebrows. "I don't know. They look like documents for Phillip's company—"

Just then Chloe's phone buzzed. She looked at it and gasped. "We have to get out of here." She ran toward the door.

I quickly grabbed the note and the folder and followed her.

Chloe took off as soon as we entered the hall. When I turned the corner, I ran straight into Jack.

I completely froze. I was unable to move or speak.

He narrowed his eyes.

Crap. *Say something, Lexi.*

"Jack, hi," I said nervously. I clutched the papers tightly against my chest.

He frowned. "What are you doing here?"

"I, um, was looking for you. We have to talk. It's urgent," I exclaimed.

His jaw tightened. "Okay, let's go to my office."

As we silently walked through the ship, I tried to come up with a good explanation for why I went against him and searched the stateroom.

"Before you say anything, let me explain," I begged as soon as we entered his office. I cleared my throat as I told him about what I'd found in the guest profiles.

"I just think it's a little unusual that Kelsey was listed as an emergency contact," I said. "Especially for Josie."

"I have to agree with you about that," Jack said. "Why would he list the woman he'd had an affair with as the person to contact if something happened?"

The more I learned about their group, the more confused I was about their relationships. I felt like I was living in an episode of *The Young and the Restless.*

I exhaled loudly. "There's something else. You're not going to like it, but I hope you'll understand after you see what I found."

I handed him the items I'd found.

"What are these?" he asked.

I looked down at the floor. "They were in Bobby and Michelle's room."

"Excuse me?"

"I know you're upset, and I completely understand, but we need to bring these to Detective LeFleur right away."

"Of course I'm upset," he said. His voice went up a few octaves. "I've told you repeatedly to let the authorities handle it."

I frowned. "So you think I should sit back and do nothing instead of helping my childhood friend?"

"I didn't say that." He paused and looked away. "I just don't want to see anything happen to you."

My pulse picked up at his admission. For a split second I wondered if Jack's urgent plea for me to stay out of the investigation was more than just professional.

Gah! I didn't want to go there. I had to stay focused.

I sat down in a chair next to his desk and folded my hands in my lap. "I wanted to leave here knowing I'd done everything I could for the family. I still wish I could've saved Phillip the same way my life was spared."

Jack gave me a curious look and sat down next to me. "What are you talking about?"

It occurred to me that I'd never told Jack about almost drowning and how the lifeguard saved my life.

"I almost drowned in the Atlantic Ocean when I was fifteen," I explained. "I was with my family, and my mother warned me about the strong current. I've always loved the water, and at that age I thought I was invincible. That is, until I felt that undertow pulling me out to sea. I still remember that helpless feeling—it was terrifying. I tried to fight it, but I became exhausted. That's when I felt two arms tighten around me. I was saved by a lifeguard, and from that day forward I knew I had to return the favor someday."

Each time I relived that memory, it felt like I was back on that beach.

"Lexi, you weren't going to save Phillip's life. He wasn't just a drowning victim."

I pursed my lips. "Everyone keeps telling me that, but no one can understand how it feels in that moment. The urgency, the adrenaline, the panic—I know Phillip was probably already gone, but what if it had been another guest?"

Jack placed his hand on my shoulder, causing another stir within me. He was close enough for me to breathe in his familiar scent, and it was divine.

Our faces were a few inches apart, and I felt an urging to move even closer. Why was his presence affecting me like this?

I jumped up from my chair before I did something I'd really regret. "I'm sorry, but I can't stand by and stay silent. That's not who I am, and I will not compromise my integrity. I have faith the truth will prevail, and if I can help make it happen, I will. I'm bringing this to Detective LeFleur with or without you."

He let out a frustrated sigh and reached for his phone. I was more determined than ever, and selfishly I needed the distraction from Jack and my growing attraction.

* * *

Detective LeFleur was waiting at the resort when we arrived. He frowned as soon as he saw me. I knew Jack would've preferred to go by himself, but I wasn't having it. I had a mission to accomplish, and he knew there was no chance he'd change my mind. Deep down, I knew he agreed with me, but he was in a tough spot with his job. I respected his position and didn't want to jeopardize that for him. He had to keep Epic Cruise Line away from scandal and keep its great reputation intact.

"Hello, Ms. Walker," Detective LeFleur said in a polite tone. "I didn't expect to see you again."

Jack held up his hand, signaling me to let him speak, which I did. "Lexi found a few things she thinks may help in the case, and she wanted to share them with you."

The detective raised his eyebrows.

"Yes." I handed him the envelope and papers.

"Where did you get these?"

I gave Jack a hopeful look.

He pursed his lips together. "They were found while packing up Bobby and Michelle's stateroom."

I let out a deep breath. I knew he was still angry, but I was so thankful he'd covered for me.

"I found the note to be very sincere. She sounds really excited to start her new life."

He pulled the card out of the envelope and read it.

"When I came across it, I thought it might be helpful if you needed something to show the relationship between the Edwards and Bobby and Michelle."

He slid the notecard back into the envelope. "Thank you, Ms. Walker. I will make a note as we continue the investigation."

"And the documents in the folder look like they have something to do with Phillip's business," I added. "Why would Bobby bring them on a vacation in the islands?"

Detective LeFleur glanced at the contents of the folder and gave a nod.

"I have a new theory," I blurted out. I'd probably crossed the line again, but I was not a quitter, so I needed to tell him what I'd told Chloe.

Jack rubbed his temples, and the detective looked frustrated.

"I think Bobby, Michelle, and Kelsey were all involved in Phillip's murder," I said. "We know there were rifts in their relationships. Maybe Bobby wanted his company back and Kelsey wanted revenge for Phillip choosing another woman."

The detective didn't say anything, so I continued.

"Kelsey told me she felt guilty about wishing something bad would happen to Phillip, and she said he was murdered. Of course she blamed Josie for everything." I paused. "Maybe their intention was to set Josie up to take the fall, but Kelsey had an attack of conscience and she was killed to keep her from telling the truth."

Judging by the detective's tired expression, I knew I needed to stop. Jack looked just as uncomfortable, so I backed off a little.

"I know I'm overstepping here, but please understand I'm trying to help this family," I insisted.

Detective LeFleur was listening, so I continued with my theory. "It's common knowledge that Phillip had strained relationships with a lot of people for various reasons. His business dealings with Bobby and his affair with Kelsey. Isn't it possible that Josie is being targeted for the same reasons everyone was against their marriage?"

The detective didn't say anything. I'm sure he was tired of my help, and it probably sounded like I was doubting his abilities to do his job. "You make several valid points, Ms. Walker. Many of which we've already considered. Well done."

What did that mean?

"You've been very helpful, but as I said earlier, we've got it under control."

In other words, he was reminding me to stay out of it.

"I understand, but I appreciate you listening," I said.

"And I appreciate your willingness to help," Detective LeFleur replied.

"I'm going to check in with my contact Ty before I head back the ship," I told Jack. "I can catch up with you later if you need to leave."

He frowned. He knew I had originally planned on talking to Josie, but I headed toward Ty's office anyway to prove that I wasn't lying to him.

I wasn't sure if he was in today, so I knocked loudly on his door.

"Come in," he called.

I popped my head in, and he jumped up from his desk as soon as he saw me.

"Lexi, what's going on? I was wondering if I'd see you today. I tried calling over to the ship, but they told me you were off."

I sighed. "The last few days have been so chaotic."

He waved me into his office. "Tell me what's going on. I left right after we spoke yesterday, and when I came in today, all hell had broken loose. Two people have died on the property in the last twenty-four hours, and one of them was one of your passengers."

I plopped down in a chair next to his desk. "Did you hear what happened?"

He held his hands up. "Bits and pieces. Management has asked that we try to keep things business as usual, so I've kept my head down and my ears open."

Ty was one of my favorite people. He was friendly and always helpful.

I explained that Phillip was one of the guests whom I'd booked on the concierge day, and I told him about the hot tub. I also told him about Josie and me reconnecting after all those years.

"Wow. What are the chances that she'd come on your ship? That's a wild story."

I nodded. "I just wish it had a different outcome. Phillip and Josie should be enjoying the islands and celebrating their new life. Unfortunately, that didn't happen."

Ty gave me a sympathetic look. "I'm so sorry, girl. That's rough."

I tilted my head back. "I want this to be over, but I feel like I should help Josie. Apparently, no one wanted Phillip to marry her. And I've been worried that I'd somehow get dragged into the investigation if they found her guilty."

He cringed. "Do you think she is?"

I shook my head. "Actually, I don't, but I'm still worried about our connection. I was with her right before we found her husband in the hot tub."

"Wow. I can't believe this all happened here at our resort."

I hung my head and nodded.

If anything, I hoped my efforts had shown Jack how dedicated I was when I put my mind to something. Of course, other people might think I was too close to this situation and feel differently. I had a feeling once we returned to Miami, I'd know my fate.

"I'll definitely keep you posted," I told Ty. "Our next itinerary with a stop here is in two weeks. Hopefully I'll be sending you more guests."

He put his hands in praying position. "Let's hope the cruise lines still want to send guests here. You should be thankful the deaths didn't happen on your ship."

He was right. The Paradise Island Resort was dealing with the fallout of this as well—Kelsey was one of their guests.

"Will you let me know if you hear anything around here?"

He leaned his head to the side. "Girl, you know I will. I always get the best gossip."

Ty stood up and gave me a hug. I was glad I'd stopped to talk to him.

As soon as I left his office, I glanced at my phone to make sure there were no calls from Jack.

So far, so good.

I made a beeline for Josie's room. It had seemed like she'd lost all hope earlier, but maybe I could help give her a little back.

CHAPTER SEVENTEEN

———

As I made my way through the hotel, more doubts crept into my mind. The detective obviously wasn't happy about my continued involvement in his case, and how far was too far? My past interaction with law enforcement had been minimal—I'd never even had a speeding ticket. Binge watching crime shows on TV certainly hadn't made me an expert.

Maybe I was overreacting to something I'd never get resolution for? Chloe was probably right about me letting it go— she loved being right.

I pushed the elevator button and waited.

Just as I was about to get on the elevator, Jack came around the corner. "I'm glad I found you. We need to have a talk."

The tone in his voice was firm and urgent. Clearly he meant business. I wondered if he was going to mention our close encounter from earlier.

"Okay."

He motioned for me to follow him.

I sighed as the elevator door shut without me inside. As much as I wanted to talk to Josie, my career was more important.

"Let's take a walk. I'm sure you know your way around this resort by now, right?" he teased.

I rolled my eyes. "Very funny."

I followed him through the large French doors that opened onto a massive terrace. There were two curved staircases that led down to a garden with the crystal blue ocean just beyond that. He trotted down the stairs, with me trailing a step behind him. As soon as we got to the bottom, Jack looked back at the resort.

"After you left, Detective LeFleur asked why you were still so concerned with the resolution of this case."

Crap. I should've left well enough alone without presenting him with my theories. I'd basically questioned his ability to do his job. I'd already rocked the boat enough, no pun intended.

"I think we should return to the ship," he demanded.

I nodded. I'd already pressed my luck for the day. Maybe he was right and I'd done everything I could do.

* * *

After we returned to the ship, Jack and I said a quick good-bye without any mention of our close encounter from earlier. I stopped by the Port Adventures office and left a message for another one of our guests. I'd booked the Dolphin Swim and Sail for them the same night I'd met Josie and Phillip. I needed to follow up and make sure they'd had a good experience. It certainly couldn't have been any worse than what happened to Phillip and Josie. Ugh. I cringed at the thought.

"Hey, Lexi," my coworker Trina said, popping her head into my office.

I sat up straight in my chair, prepared for all the questions. "Hi. Come on in. I was just checking in with a guest."

Trina stood awkwardly in the doorway. I didn't know what was going through her mind, but I assumed she'd heard about Phillip and the investigation.

"Sorry I've been MIA. I'm sure you and Caleb have been rocking it."

She sheepishly grinned. "I don't know about that. This sailing has been one of the slower ones. I booked three excursions for today, though."

"Good for you."

Trina had only been with Epic for around three months. She'd been extremely homesick at first. The first few weeks I was sure she'd never make it, but I thought she was finally getting used to life on the water.

"How's everything with you?" she asked, trying to sound casual.

Poor girl. I didn't want to leave her hanging, so I went straight for bringing up the elephant in the room.

"It's okay, Trina. I already know everyone is talking about what happened at the Paradise Island Resort."

Her shoulders relaxed slightly. "I didn't want to say anything if you weren't up for talking about it."

"It's fine."

"So is any of it true?"

I raised my eyebrows. "That depends on what you've heard."

I'd worked for this company long enough to know that things got twisted and rumors had a way of taking on lives of their own. Gossip on a cruise ship was like the game of telephone on crack.

"There are a few different rumors going around, but most of them are completely ridiculous."

I leaned back in my chair and motioned for her to sit down. "This should be fun. Let's hear them."

Trina twisted her long blonde hair then took off her tortoiseshell glasses and placed them on my desk. "The first thing I heard was that you and Mrs. Edwards are actually stepsisters and you conspired together to kill her husband. That's why you went to the Paradise Island Resort to see her."

I laughed. "That's definitely not true. Josie and I knew each other when we were kids, but I just met Phillip for the first time two nights ago."

She rolled her eyes. "I figured as much. Another rumor going around is that you and Jack Carson are romantically involved, and you've been using the Phillip Edwards death as a cover to spend time together."

I thought about the intense moments I'd shared with Jack. The rumor wasn't true, but we did have an undeniable connection. "That's also not true. There's nothing going on between Jack Carson and me."

She gave me a funny look. I could tell by her expression that she didn't believe me. "I also heard that you found Phillip Edwards in a hot tub at the resort, you tried to perform CPR, but he was already dead. And the police are investigating what really happened to him, and they don't think it was a drowning accident."

Bingo. "We have a winner."

"So, that is true?" she asked, shock in her voice. "And you're friends with the wife?"

Jack's concerns replayed through my mind. I knew he didn't want me to continue my own investigating, and I was sure I wasn't supposed to discuss the details of the case.

"We were friends in fourth grade," I told Trina. "She moved away, and I hadn't seen her since then."

"Wow. How funny that she ended up on our ship," Trina exclaimed. "I also heard another woman drowned in a hot tub at the resort. Is that true, or did someone make it up?"

I lowered my head. "Sadly, yes. Have any of the guests asked you about the rumors?"

She shook her head. "Nothing."

Good.

"I'm really sorry you had to go through that," she said.

I shrugged. "It's been rough, but I did everything I could for him. I kept going until the paramedics arrived. It was very surreal."

She gave me a sympathetic nod.

"There was one other rumor that had something to do with Mr. Edwards' best friend—I guess they came on this sailing with them."

I nodded. "What was it?"

She rolled her eyes. "Someone said they overheard the couple talking at the Paris Bar the night we set sail. Apparently they were making toasts and talking about the end of Phillip Edwards' reign? It's probably another lie."

Hmm…the end of Phillip's reign? That certainly went along with my theory.

"At least we're setting sail tomorrow. I'm sure you're ready to leave," she said, pulling me out of my thoughts.

I really was looking forward to it, which made me sad. I used to love stopping in this port. Hopefully I wasn't jaded forever.

My phone rang, interrupting our discussion. Trina stood up and pointed to the door. I gave her a quick wave.

"Port Adventures, this is Lexi," I answered.

"Hello, this is Mike Wilson. We just got back to our room and received your message."

"Hello, Mr. Wilson," I said cheerfully.

"I wanted to tell you that our family had an amazing day. The kids are already begging to come back."

That was exactly what I needed to hear. "Thank you for returning my call. That's wonderful news," I gushed.

"Absolutely, and thank you again for the recommendation. Your knowledge and customer service exceeded our expectations. We're already planning on cruising with you again."

His last comment brought tears to my eyes. I was definitely feeling overly emotional, and with good reason.

"Fantastic. One of our main goals is to make sure our guests have the best experience so they'll return," I said as I cleared my throat. "Please let me know if there's anything else I can help you with while you're on board with us."

I had a feeling of validation as I hung up the phone. I really needed that phone call tonight. It gave me hope that everything would turn out okay after all.

CHAPTER EIGHTEEN

———

The ocean air blew through my hair as I walked along the top deck of the ship. I stared out over the vast ocean that surrounded us—it was definitely one of my favorite views ever. The sun was gleaming off the ocean, which made it look like diamonds. The water was extremely calm—nothing like the last few days had been for me. I closed my eyes and let the sound of the waves soothe me. It was funny that the ocean could be so amazing and scary all at the same time. I stood and watched as the sun faded into the horizon. Just as my thoughts began to swirl, I heard a familiar voice.

"It never gets old, does it?"

I turned to my left to find Jack also staring out at the sunset. "Never."

"It's hard to believe that most people don't get to experience this every day of their lives. We're pretty lucky."

I agreed, "We are. That's why I was so worried about losing my job. I'm not ready to say good-bye to this yet."

Jack rested his arms on the railing, his gaze still focused on something in the distance. "I have a confession to make."

My pulse picked up. I had no idea what he was about to tell me. "Is it good or bad?" I asked, feeling both exhilarated and worried.

He turned toward me and reached for my waist, pulling me into him. My heart was practically beating outside of my chest. Before I knew what was happening, his lips were on mine. I wrapped my arms tightly around his neck and pulled him even closer to me.

Our kiss grew more urgent, when suddenly I heard someone calling my name. "Lexi, help me, please."

I pulled away from Jack and looked at his face.

"Ignore that. I've wanted you in my arms since the moment we met," he murmured.

"Help, please," the voice called again.

I'd never felt so torn. I wanted to stay in Jack's arms, where I felt safe. But I couldn't ignore the desperate pleas for help.

"He's dying, hurry."

I finally pried myself away from Jack and looked over the railing to the deck below, where the pool was. That's when I saw Josie kneeling with Phillip in her arms. She was shaking him and crying.

What was going on? Phillip was dead. I'd pulled him out of the water. How was he here?

"Josie," I called.

"Help me, please!" she screamed. "I didn't do it. I love my husband."

Maybe I had another chance to save him. I started to run but couldn't find a way to get to the pool.

"Lexi, please help me. You're my only friend."

"I'm trying to help," I called. "Hold on. I'm trying."

"Lexi, wake up."

I screamed and jumped up to find myself in my room with Chloe standing over me. My heart raced as I breathed heavily.

"Lexi, are you okay?"

I sat on the edge of my bed and put my hands over my face.

"That must've been some dream."

I put my hand to my chest as I tried to catch my breath.

"You kept repeating 'I'm trying' over and over. Do you remember what you were dreaming about?"

Yes, I remembered. Jack was kissing me. I didn't want to tell Chloe, even though that was the good part of the dream. "Josie was sitting next to the pool with Phillip in her arms, begging me to help her. She said I was her only friend, and I told her that I was trying to help. This is why I can't give up yet."

"Oh, honey," Chloe said. She sat next to me and put her arm around my shoulders. "Do you think you need to talk to someone? There's nothing wrong with asking for help after what you experienced."

I frowned. "You think I should talk to a therapist?"

She shrugged. "It couldn't hurt. Talking to someone may help you come to terms with what happened."

I replayed the dream in my head. "The last thing Josie said in the dream was that she didn't do it and she loved her husband."

Chloe chewed on her lip. "Dreams can be very telling."

She had no idea. "I think so, too. I was trying to stay out of it because Jack is fed up. But I still feel like something is being missed."

"And you think you can help?"

I shrugged. "I think Josie needs to know someone believes her."

Chloe didn't say anything, but I'd already made up my mind. I was going back to the Paradise Island Resort one last time. The ship was leaving port later that day. It was a few minutes after six in the morning, so I had more than enough time to see Josie and make it back to the ship.

"You're going there, aren't you?" Chloe asked finally.

"Yes, and you need to cover for me if Jack happens to call."

She groaned. "Aren't you the least bit worried? Two murders are being investigated."

Of course I was worried, but I didn't want any more nightmares like the one I'd just had. Although, I didn't mind the part with Jack's arms around me. I had never quit on anything without giving it my all, and I wasn't going to let this be the first time.

* * *

I threw on a pair of denim shorts, a white T-shirt, and a Miami Dolphins baseball cap. I borrowed Chloe's huge Gucci sunglasses. I stood in front of the mirror and stared at my reflection. Maybe I'd gone a little overboard in my efforts to go incognito. Hopefully I wouldn't bring more attention to myself with my innocent disguise.

Chloe begged and pleaded to come with me, and I refused. She needed to stay clear of the drama and cover for me here. If I was going down for interfering in a police investigation, I wasn't dragging her with me. I gave her strict instructions to tell anyone who asked that I was catching up on sleep today and wanted to be left alone. I hoped Jack wouldn't check the computer and see that I'd left the boat. I'd ask for forgiveness later if I needed to.

I was still feeling a bit shaken by the dream, mostly because of Josie and Phillip. However, my hot make-out session with Jack was also fresh on my mind.

After lacing up my tennis shoes, I slipped my ID badge into my crossbody bag. I didn't have any intention of using it once I stepped off the ship, but I was required to have it with me at all times. Of course, the one person I hoped to avoid was Detective LeFleur.

As soon I got off the ship, I walked through the Nassau welcome center. I loved going to the island. The people were lovely and welcoming. As I walked, I paused a few times to look at the shell jewelry and straw bags in the marketplace. Several sweet ladies asked if they could braid my hair, and about ten companies offered to give me a tour of the island. I stopped to breathe in the salty scent of the ocean air, and for a second I actually felt like a tourist on vacation.

I hailed a taxi to the resort by myself, something we were instructed not to do. The buddy system was highly recommended when we visited other countries, but today was going to be the exception. I nervously twisted my fingers as I stared out the window. We crossed the bridge onto Paradise Island and drove down the familiar circular driveway. The closer we got, the more nervous I felt. There was a part of me that felt terrible about going against Jack's advice. He'd been so understanding, and I'd completely disregarded his wishes. On the other hand, that dream really shook me up. It seemed like something was telling me to not give up on getting answers. I also felt like I was the only person on Josie's side. Based on what I'd heard, it was doubtful that Phillip's family would be supportive of her, even after the case was solved.

Drew was very adamant that his parents weren't terrible people, but they were going through unimaginable pain after losing their son. I'd always heard that grief made people do crazy things.

The taxi driver pulled around to the far left of the resort at my request. I didn't want to walk through the lobby in case the police were still hanging around there. After paying my fare, I adjusted my hat and walked through the gardens and toward the recreational area where Phillip had taken his last breath. It was buzzing with guests and obviously back to normal operations. Judging by the smiles and sounds, you'd never have known a man died there two days ago. Unfortunately, I'd never look at this place the same way again.

I entered the hotel through the side French doors and made a beeline for the elevator. Paranoia was setting in as I lowered my head and kept the very obvious sunglasses on. It was a good thing I wasn't famous. I sucked at being subtle.

"Hi, Lexi."

Crap. My heart sank when I heard my name. Out of all the guests on this huge property to notice me. I swung around to see Michelle. She had two coffee cups on a tray and a pastry bag in her hand.

"Hey, Michelle," I said softly.

She narrowed her eyes. "What are you doing?"

They were no longer our guests, so I couldn't use the cruise line as an excuse anymore. Not to mention I obviously wasn't working today. I didn't want to let on that I was still invested in finding out the truth, especially if Michelle had been in on it.

I took off my sunglasses and gave her a warm smile. "I met up with a friend who works here. We're leaving port tonight, and I had the day off, so I wanted to say good-bye."

She was wearing a light green cropped top with the tiniest denim shorts I'd ever seen. Her face was done up but definitely didn't have as much makeup on as she did the first day we were here.

"Oh, that's nice," she said. "By the way, Bobby and I were upset we didn't get to experience all your ship has to offer."

I nodded. "Perhaps you'll be able to cruise with us again in the future."

She sipped her coffee. "We're already planning on it. Although I think we'll do a different itinerary after this trip."

I casually looked around to make sure no one was watching our conversation. "How's Bobby doing?"

She sighed dramatically. "He's okay. I think it's finally hitting him that Phil and Kelsey are gone. I'm sure it will really sink in when we finally get home."

I still couldn't read her, but it seemed like she was trying too hard to act upset. She hadn't had any sympathy for what her boyfriend was going through when I'd seen her after Phillip's death.

She gave me a skeptical look. "Lexi, are you here to see Josie?"

Hmm...why does she want to know?

I shook my head. "I don't want to bother her. Have you spoken to her?"

"No," she said emphatically.

"I've been wondering how she's doing," I added.

She shrugged. "I couldn't say."

Michelle had certainly changed her tune.

"Oh, I thought you may have seen her."

Michelle frowned. "Yes, well, things are complicated right now. With the investigation going on, we're trying to lie low. The families are all banding together during this difficult time."

Michelle moved closer to me. "Perhaps you should do the same."

"What does that mean?" I asked.

Her comment made me uneasy.

"You don't know really know who Josie is."

I frowned. "You're right. But then again, I really don't know any of you."

A worried look spread across her face, and she moved away from me. "Um, this coffee is getting cold, so I should go. Maybe I'll see you again on another cruise."

She said good-bye and quickly headed toward the elevator while I ducked into the restroom to wait for her to be out of sight. My pulse picked up as I tried to process our conversation. It definitely seemed like she was trying to steer me away from talking to Josie. That made me even more convinced that I was doing the right thing. I took one last look at myself in the mirror, pulled my hat down above my eyes, and headed to see Josie.

CHAPTER NINETEEN

————

I'd taken a few yoga classes from our ship's instructor, Elsa. She was world renowned for Vinyasa, Bikram, and another form of practice I couldn't pronounce. At the time, all I'd cared about was getting my body to twist into some of those impossible poses. Today I wished I'd paid more attention to the lessons on breathing.

On the way to Josie's room, I tried to catch my breath, but my nerves were getting the best of me. The last thing I needed was to be found hyperventilating outside her room.

As soon as I arrived, I knocked loudly on the door.

What if she wasn't there? It wasn't like she had anywhere else to be, and I was pretty sure the police weren't letting her leave yet.

"Who is it?" she called through the door.

"Josie, it's me, Lexi."

She didn't respond. Was she ignoring me?

"Josie?"

"Lexi, why are you here?"

Well, that wasn't the greeting I expected. "Can we talk for a few minutes? I promise I'll leave you alone after that."

I waited for her to open the door or at least say something. Hopefully I hadn't come all this way for nothing.

Just when I was beginning to think she wasn't going to respond, the door opened. I was pleasantly surprised to see she looked better than yesterday. She still wasn't the same person I'd met a few days ago, but she definitely looked more put together. She was wearing clothes that actually fit and had makeup on.

"I don't have anything else to say. My attorney advised me not to talk about Phillip's or Kelsey's deaths." Her face twisted at the mention of her husband.

The poor woman had already been through so much, and I was about to make it worse. Hopefully the fact that someone believed her would help.

"I understand." I paused and folded my arms. "I was actually advised not to talk to you, either. But I haven't been able to stop thinking about everything that's happened, and then I had a really strange dream."

She leaned against the doorframe. "What kind of dream?"

I looked up and down the hall. "I'd feel much more comfortable talking about this in private," I said softly. I didn't know if her room was being watched or not. It didn't matter, though. It wasn't the kind of conversation I wanted to have out in the open.

She hesitated for a few seconds then waved me inside. "Tell me about this dream you had. Was it about Phillip?" she asked before she even closed the door.

I immediately launched into the details of my dream with Phillip and her. I didn't mention watching the sunset with Jack or our kiss because it had nothing to do with why I was there.

"I don't know if it was some sort of message or my subconscious dealing with everything. Whatever the reason, I woke up today realizing I needed to be there for you. I can't change the fact that I couldn't save Phillip, and I'll always be sorry for that, but maybe there's something else I can do. Either way, I wanted to tell you that I believe you."

Tears filled Josie's eyes as she put her hands on her face. "Thank you for saying that. You have no idea how horrible it feels to be so isolated. I've been in this room for two days, and I'm afraid to leave or talk to anyone. That's why I said you shouldn't be here."

I sighed as I tried to figure out the best way to tell her what I think happened. "I understand why you feel that way, and with good reason."

A pained expression spread across her face. "I guess I'm on my own from now on."

I took a deep breath. "I'm so sorry, Josie."

"Phillip cheated on me with Kelsey," she said with tears in her eyes.

My mouth dropped open at her admission. "You knew about it?"

She squeezed the bridge of her nose. "I knew she was in love with him, so I had my suspicions all along, but I didn't want to accept it. No one wants to admit that the person they love could hurt them so deeply. I thought when Phillip married me, it meant he ultimately chose me over her. It always bothered me the way he wouldn't cut ties, using their family relationships as an excuse. Remember how I told you I begged him to tell her not to come here?"

I nodded.

"I think there was a part of him that didn't want to let her go." She looked away. "I knew she was angry at him for marrying me. I think she wanted to punish him for choosing me."

I thought about the argument I'd witnessed at the party. I finally told Josie what I'd overheard. "I'm sorry I didn't tell you sooner. I just didn't want to add to your pain. You were going through enough."

She held her hand out to me. "Please don't apologize. I feel bad that you got mixed up in this mess. I'm sure you wish we had never reconnected."

I shook my head. "That's not true. Despite everything that's happened, I'm glad I saw you again."

She gave me a half smile.

"Anyway, the last thing I heard Kelsey say was that she hoped karma would catch up to him and that he'd get what he deserved. Then when I spoke to her, she said she wished she'd never said those things to him." I paused. "Which brings me to my theory. I actually think Bobby and Michelle drugged Phillip and Kelsey knew about it. When Kelsey called me, she was hysterical and said Phillip had been murdered. Maybe she was going to confess but they killed her before she could."

She held up her hand and shook her head. "No, Bobby and Phillip had their share of problems, but I truly don't believe he'd do something like this."

I tightened my jaw, remembering the things Bobby had said about Josie. "You know he's not your friend, right? Michelle isn't either."

She snorted. "Yeah. He was another one who didn't want Phillip to marry me. He was good at pretending, though. I thought Michelle was genuine, but I guess I was wrong. I feel really stupid because I thought befriending her could help to change Bobby's opinion of me."

My heart really went out to Josie. From what I could see, she wanted nothing more than to be happy with Phillip. She even went as far as becoming friends with Michelle in hopes it would bridge a gap between the men.

She started laughing and shook her head. "You know what the worst part is—deep down I knew what was really going on, but I wouldn't admit it to myself. Phillip was torn between doing what his family wanted and craving independence. He had that with me, but he could never separate himself from the control they had over him."

Everything about their strange group dynamic was starting to make sense, but my mind kept going back to Bobby and Michelle.

Josie rubbed her temple with her finger and closed her eyes. I could see how difficult it was for her to talk about Phillip's betrayal. Even though she looked better than the last time I'd seen her, the light she'd had that night on the ship had dimmed.

"Josie, why are you giving Bobby the benefit of the doubt?" I asked.

She shook her head. "I'm not. I still think Kelsey killed Phillip. She hated him for choosing me."

In my mind, that was still a possibility, based on her phone call to me and how other people claimed she was unstable.

"I think you could be partly right, but if that's the case, she didn't act alone," I told her. "However, I wonder if she knew the truth about Phillip's death and it cost her her life."

Josie folded her arms tightly against her chest and stared into space. "Do you want to know what Madeline said to me a few minutes before my wedding ceremony?"

Madeline? Oh yeah, she was Phillip's mother.

"She told me I'd regret marrying her son. Our marriage would never last and that he'd always loved Kelsey. I was literally about to walk out in front of a hundred people when she whispered that in my ear. It took every ounce of strength I had to make it down the aisle and through the service without losing it. Who does that to a bride during what should be the happiest moment of her life?"

"Did anyone hear her say it?" I asked.

"Oh no, she's very sly. She pretended to give me a hug at the same time. Then she ran off to her little clique and put on a big act for all the guests."

Damn. I'd heard of evil in-laws, but these people were off the charts.

"I probably should have bailed out at that moment because she didn't stop there, either. The reason I was so upset at the pool party was because Phillip and I had gotten into an argument after receiving a text from his parents. They specifically wanted me to know they'd be monitoring all the bank accounts to make sure I wasn't embezzling. I kept telling myself I could ignore the issues with them and enjoy my vacation, but it was so hard. I left him to take a walk, and when I came back to the pool, I saw you..." She trailed off.

I gave her a sympathetic nod. "So obviously someone else was with him after you left," I said.

The color drained from her face. "I shouldn't have taken that walk. I let Madeline and Andrew get to me instead of just ignoring the message. He kept telling me not to pay any attention to them. Maybe if I hadn't left, he'd still be alive."

I put my hand on her shoulder as I tried to offer some kind of comfort.

In my mind I replayed the events prior to his death that I was sure about.

There was the heated discussion between Phillip and Kelsey. And Josie said she and Phillip had an argument about his parents. Josie left to take a walk, and during that time Phillip ended up in the hot tub.

I watched as Josie twisted the massive, sparkling diamond ring that remained on her left hand. I could see the pain in her eyes. She'd lost so much in a short amount of time. I couldn't fathom how alone she felt at that moment.

"I should've listened to my mom," Josie said a few seconds later. "She asked me over and over if I wanted to go through with my marriage. What's that old saying? Mothers know best?"

She walked to the minibar and poured herself a glass of wine. Yikes, it was definitely a bit early for wine. "My poor mother has no idea what's happening. I'm so worried about how this is going to affect her."

I remembered Josie saying she told her mother not to come down here. I didn't know the details of her mother's illness, but I knew what stress could do to a person.

"I chose to ignore the truth about Phillip," she continued. "I was living in a dream world, completely blinded by love. I believed he loved me as much as I loved him, but now I don't think he ever did. How can you love someone and betray them? Look where that betrayal got him. His actions destroyed everything."

I didn't know how to answer her question. I understood why Josie wanted to talk about it, but I was eager to figure out what I was missing. As the clock ticked, it was closer to the time the ship was scheduled to leave port. I had to be back on time.

She took a long sip of her wine and wiped her mouth with the back of her hand.

"You know, even Drew tried to warn me about Phillip after we got engaged," she said.

"He did?" I exclaimed.

She held up her hand. "Well, not in so many words. He just told me that Phillip was a complicated person and that I'd have my hands full."

Something about her statement bothered me. What about Drew? Did he know more than he was letting on? Maybe he knew what Kelsey and Bobby had done. He'd mentioned the tumultuous relationships his brother had with other people. Was he covering for Kelsey or worse...?

Josie threw back the remaining contents of her glass like she was taking a shot and reached for the bottle, so I took the empty glass out of her hand.

"Maybe you should drink some water instead," I suggested.

She frowned as she plopped down on a chair. "You're probably right. Lexi, it's so surreal that you're here," she said. "You look the same as I remember. Older of course, but it kind of feels like I went back in time."

I nodded as her face fell.

"I wish I'd never had to move away. Life was difficult for my mom and me. We struggled for most of my life. That's another reason Phillip's parents didn't think I wasn't good enough for their family."

The sound of a knock on the door startled me. Josie jumped to her feet, and a look of panic spread across her face. My heart began to race. Did someone know I was here? Maybe Jack called the resort looking for me?

"Should I answer it?" she whispered. "I could just pretend I'm asleep."

The sound of a second knock made both of us jump. Josie tiptoed to the door and peered through the peephole.

Maybe I'd made a big mistake coming here, but it didn't matter because it was too late now.

"It's Drew," she said as she exhaled loudly. "Oh, thank goodness."

Drew entered the room and stopped dead in his tracks as soon as he saw me.

"Hello, Lexi," he said politely. "Is everything okay?"

I wasn't sure what to say or how to explain why I was here. But honesty was the best policy, and I was here to help my friend.

"I came back to the resort to check on Josie. Our ship is scheduled to leave port shortly, and I wanted to say good-bye."

Josie suddenly started crying. Her sobs seemed to grow louder and louder. "I'm so scared, Drew. You know I would never hurt Phil or anyone else. Why is this happening to me? Please tell me what to do."

"I'm so sorry, Josie," he said.

"This is all Kelsey's fault," she insisted. "I know it. She had to be behind all of this. There's no other explanation."

She continued crying. Her performance was practically Oscar-worthy. Although I knew those tears weren't fake. Every bit of emotion Josie was expressing was real and raw. It was really happening to her.

"I've never felt so alone in my whole life," she said.

"You're not alone. I care about you, Josie," Drew said softly. "What Kelsey and Phillip did to you was awful," he stated. "I would've never treated you that way."

I watched as Josie's face twisted.

"You knew about their affair too?" Josie asked.

Drew looked back and forth between us. I suddenly felt extremely uncomfortable.

"This probably isn't the time to talk about it," he said, shooting a glance at me.

"You can say anything in front of Lexi. We've been friends forever."

It was kind of true. Although it'd been a very long time since we'd seen each other.

Drew sighed loudly. "My brother was never going to change. He said he wanted to be a better person, but I knew him too well. One by one he continued to hurt everyone who mattered—Bobby, you, me. I told him not to get married if he was going to continue cheating on you. He finally ended it with Kelsey, but I believe your marriage put her over the edge."

"If you care about me, why are you letting your parents blame me for Phillip's death?" Josie screamed.

"I do care about you, Josie. More than you know," he shouted. "It wasn't supposed to end like this."

There was an edge in his voice I'd never heard before.

"I wanted you to see what kind of a man my brother was and be there for you. You wouldn't open your eyes to see what was in front of you the whole time. Phillip didn't deserve you."

"Drew, what are you saying?" Josie demanded.

Just then it hit me. Kelsey hadn't drugged Phillip. Drew had. It was him all along.

CHAPTER TWENTY

———

I gasped out loud and quickly covered my mouth. It was Drew. That explained why he warned Josie about his brother. The man was in love with his brother's wife. I was actually watching a real love triangle play out in front of me. *Was it a crime of passion all along?*

He gave me a strange look, which I tried to ignore. I glanced at Josie, who looked overwhelmed and confused.

I needed to find Detective LeFleur and tell him what I'd heard. The problem was Drew hadn't admitted he'd killed his brother yet. There was a part of me that wanted to leave and never look back—I'd move on with my life and enjoy the career I loved. But Josie was truly alone, and she needed me now more than ever.

I tried to swallow the lump that was in my throat.

"Josie, maybe we should take a walk. Some fresh ocean air might do you some good," I said, reaching for her arm.

"It's okay. I'll look after her," Drew said protectively. "But maybe you should be getting back to the ship."

Was he trying to get rid of me?

"You mean like you looked after your brother?" I asked.

Josie looked confused. If Drew was involved, I had to find out now. I was definitely stepping out on a limb. Hopefully I wouldn't fall.

"What are you talking about?" Drew asked with an edge in his voice.

"It was you, wasn't it?"

Josie looked back and forth between Drew and me.

"I had a feeling there was more to Phillip's and Kelsey's deaths," I told him. "At first I thought Bobby was the most likely suspect. He had a good reason to want revenge on Phillip and kept avoiding questioning. I even thought Michelle could be involved because of her sudden friendship with Josie."

I didn't know where this burst of courage came from, but it was my last chance. It had to end. Drew nervously ran his hand through his hair.

"Lexi, what are you saying?" Josie asked.

"It was you. You killed your brother to get him out of the picture so you could be with Josie."

"What?" Josie shouted.

Drew was silent and breathing heavily. "You don't know any of us. My brother brought nothing but shame and misery, and everyone still put him on a pedestal. My parents, Kelsey, and then you," he said, pointing at Josie.

"Everyone worshiped Phillip, and he didn't deserve it." He paused and clenched his jaw. "You were too good for him. I really thought you were different, that you'd be able to see through him, but I was wrong. I've had to make excuses for him my whole life, and I was tired of it. I told him to end things with you and be with Kelsey, but he wouldn't listen. He kept Kelsey within reach just in case things didn't work out with you. You were so head over heels for him, and he knew it. I'd had enough of his antics, so I brought him a drink when he was sitting in the hot tub…"

"And you put Rohypnol in that drink."

Drew's face turned red, and he clenched his fists. "I couldn't stand seeing him with you anymore," he yelled. "He was rambling on about you overreacting to something our parents said. I brought him a shot, told him he needed to relax."

"So you killed him?" Josie asked, her voice barely over a whisper.

He looked at Josie and nodded.

"But I did it for you, so you could be free of him and his lies."

I felt like I was watching Drew come apart before my eyes. His face was flushed, and he seemed disoriented.

"And what about Kelsey?" I asked.

He didn't take his eyes off of Josie as he continued talking. "After you and Kelsey had that argument, she called me to ask for help. I met her out by the pool. She was blaming you for Phillip's death, and I told her it wasn't your fault. Somehow she figured everything out—my feelings for you and that I'd drugged my brother."

"So you drowned her?" I said.

"She was going to destroy everything," he shouted. "I had to stop her from going to the authorities. She was drunk, and she fell into the hot tub…" He trailed off. "I had no choice but to keep her quiet."

Josie shook her head in disgust. "I can't…"

"I even told my parents that I thought she could be involved in Phillip's death and then took her own life, but they didn't believe it. That's when everything started getting complicated. They insisted that you had to be the person who killed their precious Phillip so you could get your hands on everything. I tried to reason with them, but they wouldn't hear it. I tried to help you."

My head was spinning at his admission. The lies obviously had become too much for him to bear. The walls were closing in on him, and he knew it. I didn't know what would happen next, but I needed to get to the detective.

"You have to come clean to the police," I said. "If you care about Josie as much as you say, you'll tell the truth."

Drew didn't respond. His eyes had become cold and empty. "It doesn't matter anymore."

Josie and I glanced at each other. Her face was red and swollen from her tears. She looked as uncomfortable as I felt. I didn't know what to do next. I thought I could try to make a run for it, but was it safe to leave her alone with him?

Josie moved closer to Drew. "It matters to me. I wish I'd known who Phillip really was. I was caught under his spell like everyone else."

She stood right in front of him and reached out to take his hand. He looked down as she gently cradled his hand in hers.

Holy crap. What was she doing?

"I understand why you did it, and I'm sorry it took me so long to realize who Phillip really was." Josie's voice was so soothing, even I was captivated.

Drew's eyes fixated on her, and that's when I realized how deep his feelings were.

I figured out what Josie was doing, though—she was trying to distract him so I could leave.

I slowly started to move toward the door, and just when it was within reach, Drew ran toward me. "I don't think so," he yelled and moved to block the door.

I stopped in my tracks. I was so terrified, my feet felt like they were glued to the carpet. This man had just killed his own brother and a close family friend. I had no idea what he'd do to me. I was frozen with more fear than I'd ever experienced in my life, even more than when I almost drowned in the violent ocean.

"Please let her go," Josie begged. "This is about me. She doesn't have anything to do with this."

Drew snorted. "Let her go? So she can go to the police and tell them everything? I don't think so."

"Lexi won't tell," Josie pleaded. "She'll get on her ship and never look back. You and I can figure this out. We can convince the police it was Kelsey. We can finally be together."

Drew's face softened slightly. "I wish that were possible, but it's too late for us. It didn't have to be this way for you, Lexi. Your involvement and nonstop questions complicated things more than they had to be."

I still couldn't move because the fear was all-encompassing. I should've listened to Jack and stayed away. I wondered if I'd ever see him or anyone else again.

"Drew, please stop," Josie pleaded, wrapping her arms around his neck. "I'll do whatever you want. Just talk to me."

For a brief moment Drew seemed completely mesmerized by Josie's actions, so I backed away and reached for my phone, which was in my back pocket. I frantically searched for the detective's number.

I hit the call button and kept my hands behind my back.

"It's okay, Josie," I said loudly.

"Drew, please let her go," she pleaded.

My heart was racing as I prayed the detective could hear what was going on.

"What are you doing?" Drew asked sharply.

I shrugged. "Nothing."

He walked toward me and yanked my arm from behind my back. A wave of pain shot through my body. He grabbed my phone and threw it against the wall, shattering it.

Before I knew what was happening, Josie lunged for him, and he fell to the floor.

"Lexi, go."

As I started to make a run for it, something stopped me. I couldn't leave her with him. Poor Josie had been through enough, but I knew I had to get help. It was a difficult choice, but I had to try.

"You're not going anywhere," Drew said, grabbing my ankle and pulling me to the floor, sending another jolt of pain through my body as I hit the hardwood floor.

"Drew, stop," Josie yelled.

I tried to crawl away, but he had a tight grip on my leg. As I struggled to pull away, the door suddenly flew open before I could get there. Two armed officers stormed the room, and one of them yelled to stay down. I followed instructions and waited, not knowing if they were talking to me. There were a few crashes and what sounded like struggling. I had no idea what was happening or if anyone was hurt.

I closed my eyes tighter and thought about all the places I'd rather be. At home with my parents, on the ship with my friends, with Jack—

"Ms. Walker, are you okay?"

I was afraid to look up.

"It's okay. You're safe," Detective LeFleur said.

When I finally lifted my head, it took a second for me to get my bearings. Josie was on the floor, sobbing with her hands covering her eyes. Drew was lying on the floor in handcuffs with two officers standing over him.

"It was Drew. He killed Phillip and Kelsey," I shouted.

"Are you hurt?" the detective asked.

I shook my head slowly. "No, just very shaken up."

He gave me a sympathetic look. "I'll give you a few minutes to collect yourself. Then I'll need to take your statement."

I pulled my knees into my chest and wrapped my arms tightly around them. I was too overwhelmed to cry or ask questions or even stand up. I rested my head on my arms and breathed deeply. *Was it finally over?* I wanted to cry, but my emotions were all over the place.

A few seconds later, I felt a hand on my shoulder. I looked up to see it belonged to Jack.

Before I could think about what I was doing, I scrambled to my feet and threw my arms around his neck. That's when the tears started flowing as his arms tightened around my body. At that moment, there was no place I'd rather have been.

"It's alright," he whispered. The sound of his voice was like music to my ears. My mind was racing with my thoughts, questions, and emotions, but I didn't say anything. I let Jack hold me, and I didn't care if it was inappropriate or that I could lose my job. The only things that mattered were I was alive and everyone knew the truth. I continued to cry as if every bit of emotion I'd ever felt was escaping my body.

When I finally pulled away, Jack didn't loosen his grip around my waist.

"How did you know I was here?" I asked as I wiped under my eyes.

"Chloe came to me. She got worried because you hadn't returned to the ship."

Thank goodness for Chloe. I was so lucky to have her as a friend.

"After Chloe told me you were gone, I contacted Detective LeFleur, and he said he hadn't seen you. I was concerned, so I came to look for you. When I arrived, he told me he'd just gotten a call from you."

"It was Drew," I exclaimed. "He was in love with Josie. He killed his brother and drowned Kelsey because she somehow figured it out."

I shuddered at the ordeal I'd just experienced.

"I can't believe I never suspected him. I guess you were right. I was in way over my head."

Jack looked at me dubiously. "That's not true. You insisted on coming back here again and again. You went against my suggestions and that of Detective LeFleur. You continued to dig, ask questions. You pointed out that Phillip had strained relationships with Bobby and Kelsey, and you were right. It's not your fault you didn't know his brother was in love with Josie."

I looked over at Josie, who was talking to the detective. A feeling of relief washed over me. I was glad I could help her after all she'd been through.

I sucked in a breath to hold back more tears. Jack rubbed his hand up and down my back. Something about his touch was so comforting. I couldn't let myself get used to it, though. Even if I had a job after this, Jack was still off-limits. Getting involved with him would make things more complicated than they already were.

"You don't have to worry now," he reminded me.

Detective LeFleur finished talking to Josie and joined Jack and me. "Are you ready to give your statement, Ms. Walker?"

I held my head up high. "Where do you want me to start?"

"How about when you arrived at the hotel today?"

I explained every detail to Detective LeFleur, starting with my plan to go to the resort and stay out of his sight. I told him about talking to Josie and believing that Bobby was covering for Kelsey.

"As soon as Drew said that his brother didn't deserve Josie, the pieces started to come together for me. He admitted to giving Phillip a shot and drowning Kelsey to keep her quiet. He seemed so empty and desperate… I think he realized the truth had caught up to him."

Detective LeFleur made notes as I spoke.

"He said Kelsey blamed Josie for Phillip's death and asked him for help. Drew told us everything he did was for Josie."

Jack shook his head in disbelief. Not that I blamed him. It was hard to fathom that someone could use love as a reason to kill another human being.

"There were so many different factors to this case," Detective LeFleur said. "Drew Edwards was very helpful and open throughout the entire investigation. The case grew more difficult after Kelsey Clark was found dead."

I recalled my conversation with Kelsey the night before she died and how distraught she'd been. I felt sorry for her. She was also a victim of both Phillip and Drew.

I was so relieved it was all over, and I couldn't wait to get back to the ship.

Wait! What time was it?

"Jack, what about the ship?" I exclaimed in a panic. "We're supposed to be leaving."

He put his hand on my shoulder, which made my heart flutter. Every time the man touched me, it caused a chain reaction. "It's alright. The crew is aware of the situation. If we don't make it, we'll meet them back in Miami."

I felt sick to my stomach. I'd been advised to stay out of the investigation, and I hadn't listened.

"Lexi?" Josie's voice dragged me out of my thoughts. As soon as I looked at her, she started crying and threw her arms around me.

It was in that moment I knew Josie and I were meant to see each other again. I'd always believed people came into our lives for a reason. Who would have thought two little girls in the same fourth-grade class would reconnect and go through such a harrowing ordeal? Josie needed a true friend, and maybe I was that friend. I knew we'd always be connected, not just because of our history but because of what we'd just been through.

Chloe insisted intense situations brought people together, and she was right. Of course she was referring to Jack and me, but that remained to be seen.

"How can I ever begin to thank you for everything you've done for me?" she said, letting go of me. "I'm so grateful we found each other again."

I squeezed her hands. "You don't need to thank me. And I feel the same way."

She sighed and looked over at Drew.

One of the officers helped him to his feet and escorted him out of the room. He didn't say a word or try to resist. He just had a blank stare on his face. His expression was emotionless and eerie.

Josie didn't take her eyes off Drew as they led him out.

"Are you okay?" I asked her. That was a dumb question, because I knew she wasn't. The last few days had been a complete nightmare, and she still had to go home and bury her husband.

"No, but I will be, thanks to you."

I glanced at Jack, who flashed me a warm smile.

"Mr. Carson, I can't even begin to thank you for everything you and Epic Cruise Line have done for me," Josie said as she placed her hands on her heart.

"You're very welcome. I'll hope you'll consider sailing with us in the future."

She nodded. "I'd like that, especially knowing I have a friend here."

I hoped so.

"My mom's never been on a cruise. Maybe I'll bring her," Josie said thoughtfully.

"Absolutely," Jack replied. "Let us know, and we'll make sure you're taken care of."

Detective LeFleur interrupted our conversation and asked to speak to Josie again. She gave me another hug and followed him away, leaving Jack and me alone.

"So, how much trouble am I in?" I asked.

He folded his arms. "Not that much."

I raised my eyebrows. Hopefully he wasn't just trying to be nice and give me the bad news later.

"Are you ready to go? We'll make it if we leave now."

Relief brought a smile to my lips. "Yes. I've never been more ready."

Jack told Detective LeFleur we needed to leave. We quickly headed for the elevator, when Bobby stepped out.

He stopped in his tracks as soon as he saw me. "What's happening?" Bobby exclaimed with a look of horror on his face. "What's all the commotion, and why was Drew in handcuffs?"

I glanced at Jack. A wave of guilt washed over me for believing he'd actually hurt his friends.

"You should probably speak to Detective LeFleur. He can give you all the details," Jack said. I was glad he spoke up as I was emotionally spent and didn't want to get into it with Bobby.

Jack stepped into the waiting elevator, and I followed. I turned around to face Bobby and held the door open with my hand.

"Just so you know, Josie is a good person, and she really did love Phillip. You should pass that information on to your families."

Bobby's face turned pale, and the elevator doors closed before he could respond.

"I think you gave him something to think about," Jack said a few seconds later.

I shrugged. "Good. I just hope Josie's going to be okay. I feel bad that she has to go back and face those awful people. You wouldn't believe the things they did to her."

The corner of Jack's mouth curled up.

"What?"

"I was thinking about how lucky Josie was that you were here," he said. "You're pretty incredible."

Hopefully my blushing wasn't too obvious.

"I'm glad you're safe," he added.

We both grew quiet but didn't take our eyes off each other. He opened his mouth to say something else, when the elevator doors opened.

Jack looked at his phone. "We'd better hurry."

"Do you think we'll make it back in time?" I asked worriedly.

"I hope so."

CHAPTER TWENTY-ONE

———

Jack and I raced across the gangway just as they were about to close the doors. I almost dropped down and kissed the floor until I saw Chloe pacing back and forth.

"Lexi!" she shouted as she rushed toward me. "You nearly gave me a heart attack. I should've never let you leave by yourself."

I gave her a hug. "I know. I'm sorry I worried you."

"What happened? You left hours ago."

I sighed. There was so much to tell her, I didn't know where to start. I glanced at Jack, who stood awkwardly off to the side.

"I need to give an update to the ship officers," Jack said.

My stomach twisted at the thought.

"You should get some rest, and we'll catch up later." He turned to Chloe. "I trust you'll keep an eye on her?"

She linked her arm with mine. "Yes, of course. I won't let her jump ship again."

He started to walk away.

"Jack, wait a second," I said as I ran to catch up to him. We stood a few feet away from each other. There were crew members all around, and it definitely wasn't the place to have a private moment. "I wanted to say thank you for coming to get me and for being so understanding."

He gave me a nod before turning down the hall. As I watched him leave, I considered running after him and actually making the wonderful part of my dream come to life. According to Trina, most of the ship thought we were involved anyway.

"Let's get you back to our room," Chloe demanded. She sounded like a concerned mother, but I didn't object. As we walked, Chloe talked a mile a minute. She told me about going to see Jack when I hadn't returned and how the staff was talking about the ship leaving the Bahamas without us.

When we got back to our room, I immediately got into the shower. As I let the steaming hot water pour over me, I replayed everything that had happened at the resort. The fact I'd just survived something so unimaginable didn't seem real. I thought about Josie and what she faced upon returning home, but it was better than being convicted of a crime she didn't commit. I had a feeling she would rise out of this tragedy a stronger, more capable person.

When I got out of the shower, I wrapped a towel around my hair and wiped the steam off the mirror. I'd never been more grateful to be in my tiny bathroom on this beautiful ship.

There was so much to think about, and I still faced a lot of questions about my own future. For tonight I was safe, and hopefully I'd sleep better knowing justice would be served.

* * *

"I can't believe Drew was in love with Josie," Chloe exclaimed. "Think about it—first Phillip had an affair with Kelsey, and now that. It's just like something you'd see in a movie."

Of course Chloe wanted every detail, so I relived my horrific experience all over again while she got ready for her performance.

"Do you want me to get my shift covered tonight?" she asked for the hundredth time. "I think I should stay. Jack told me I needed to look after you."

I shook my head. "You're not skipping your show," I insisted. "I don't need a babysitter."

She laughed. "I'm not so sure. You ran off to the island by yourself today, and look what you got yourself into."

Ugh. Did she have to remind me?

Even though Jack said I wasn't in trouble, I was concerned about what I faced after the dust settled. There had to be some kind of reprimand, or I'd at least be written up for almost missing the boat. Not to mention getting myself even deeper into the Edwards family drama.

"I'll be fine. I just need a good night's sleep." Hopefully I wouldn't have any more nightmares. Although I wouldn't mind dreaming of watching the sunset with Jack again.

"By the way, Jack was really worried about you when I told him you were gone. For a second, I thought he might jump overboard and swim to you."

I rolled my eyes. "Very funny."

She shrugged. "It's the truth," she said with a coy smile. "Maybe you should call him and let him know you're okay. I'm sure he's still concerned."

"Thanks for the advice. Isn't it time for you to get to work?"

She laughed. "Okay, I'll be back as soon as I'm finished. Try to rest, and don't try to leave the boat."

"Thanks, Mom," I teased.

As soon as she left, I dried my hair and then crawled between the soft, warm covers. It was only seven o'clock, but I felt like I'd been up for days. I stared at the ceiling and finally let the gentle motion of the boat rock me to sleep.

* * *

I was jolted from my slumber by the sound of my phone ringing. I scrambled to answer it. I didn't know what time it was, but Chloe hadn't returned from her show yet.

"Hello?"

"Hi, Lexi. I'm sorry to call so late."

It was Josie. I rubbed my eyes and sat up. "No, it's fine. How are you?"

I listened as she told me she'd spoken to Phillip's parents and they'd agreed to call a truce for the funeral. She said it helped when she told them she wanted a clean break without any of the Edwards family money.

"I'm also going to make sure Bobby gets the company back," she added. "There's so much to think about. And as difficult as it's going to be, I need to figure out how to start my life over."

"Of course," I said. "I'd imagine it's going to take some time."

"Yes." She paused. "I really did love him, despite what everyone thinks."

Poor Josie. I wished she didn't feel like she had to constantly defend herself.

"I know you did."

It sounded like she wanted to move forward from the tragic events that had just taken place, and I couldn't have been happier for her.

"Anyway, as soon as I get settled, I'd like to take my mother on a cruise," she said.

"Well, you know where to come when you're ready," I told her.

She laughed. "I sure do. Thank you, Lexi, for everything."

I ended the call and stared at the ceiling. I looked forward to what the future held in store. I just hoped I'd be enjoying it on the open seas. One thing I'd learned over the last four days was that the possibilities were endless.

* * *

The sun was just rising when I opened my eyes. I looked over to see Chloe still fast asleep with her eye mask on. I must've been in a deep sleep the night before, because I hadn't heard her come in. I looked out the window to see the familiar Port of Miami. It was debarkation day for this group of passengers, and soon we'd be welcoming a whole new group on board. This was the wildest and longest four-night cruise I'd ever been on, and I was beyond happy it was over.

As much as I wanted to go back to sleep, I knew I had to get up and start my day. I assumed I was facing many questions and meetings and was prepared to face whatever was in store for me with confidence and integrity. I had no regrets about my actions over the last four days.

I sat up on the side of the bed and stretched my arms above my head. I got dressed quickly and quietly, putting on a white peasant blouse with a pair of black pants. I ran a brush through my hair and put on some makeup. My nerves were starting to kick in, so I gave myself a pep talk. I didn't know what to expect, but I was ready to face the music.

I snuck out of my room without waking Chloe, but I did leave her a note letting her know where I was going. I was pretty sure she thought I was a flight risk, and I'd worried her enough the day before.

I made my way through the ship, saying good-bye to guests who were preparing to leave the ship. There was always a drastically different vibe on debarkation day. Vacation was over for them, and it was time to get back to real life. I was sad I didn't get to know most of our guests on this sailing, but I knew I'd made a friend for life in Josie.

I stopped outside of Jack's office to collect myself before seeing him. I knew I needed to talk to Javier about my lifeguard position, but I wanted to check in with Jack first in case he had information I should know. I knocked loudly on his door, hoping he was there.

"Yes," he called.

I opened the door and peeked my head in.

"Good morning," he said, sounding surprised to see me. "I figured you'd be still sleeping. How was your night?" He was wearing his glasses, a crisp black button-down shirt, and black slacks. Somehow he looked completely rested and as handsome as ever.

"Good." I stood awkwardly in the doorway. There was so much I wanted to say, but the pounding in my chest was distracting me. *Why was I so nervous?* The last few days had been such a whirlwind, I felt like I was still on edge. If I'd made it through that experience, I could make it through anything.

I walked toward his desk and sat in one of the chairs. I had to take that opportunity to ask him if I still had a job. "Jack, I'm just going to get to the point. Do I still have a job with Epic Cruise Line?"

He gave me a puzzled look.

"I know people talk and rumors begin from less than what I've dealt with the past few days. And didn't you come to our ship to shake things up and build new teams?"

Jack was quiet for a few seconds. "Lexi, I can't speak of your lifeguard position, but I can assure you that I have no plans to remove you from Port Adventures. Especially after what I've seen during this sailing."

Hearing him say that caused a feeling of relief to wash over me.

"If anything, you showed me how much you care about our guests. You're the type of staff member who will set us apart from our competitors. If only our ships were full of people like you."

I felt tears threatening to spill out at any second, but I refused to have another meltdown in front of him. "Thank you for saying that," I said softly. "I'm meeting with Javier this morning, and I'm extremely nervous," I continued. "I haven't spoken to my parents, and they have no idea about anything. If I'm getting fired, I need to let them know. I don't have an apartment, so I'll need to stay with them until I figure out my next step."

Jack motioned for me to stop my rambling. "First of all, you need to take a few deep breaths," he instructed.

I did as he asked.

"Lexi, you're not fired," he said firmly.

As soon as he said those words, I felt like the weight of the world was lifted off my shoulders.

"You may not have realized it yet, but you're a hero."

Hero? That was definitely a bit of a stretch. "Very funny. I don't think so—"

"You don't give yourself enough credit," he insisted. "Think about everything you've done over the last few days. You jumped into a hot tub and tried to save a man from drowning. You offered assistance and support to our guests and their loved ones during a very traumatic time. Then to top it off, you put your life on the line to help to solve two murders. That sounds pretty amazing to me."

I felt myself blush. Jack definitely knew exactly what to say to get a reaction out of me.

"As far as I'm concerned, you're an asset to Epic Cruise Line, and like I've said, this company needs more people who care as much as you do."

Tears continued to threaten my eyes, and I quickly dabbed the corners with my fingertips. "Sorry," I told him.

"Are you sure you're okay?"

I exhaled. "Believe it or not, I am. I'm ready for things to return to normal. I want to interact with new guests and plan experiences they'll remember forever."

He chuckled. "That's exactly what I expected you to say."

We both grew quiet.

"Anyway, I'm sure you have tons of work to catch up on," I said. I rose to my feet and walked toward the door, but just as I was about to leave, Jack stopped me.

"There's one issue we might have to discuss before getting back to normal," he said.

I gave him a questioning look.

"You really must reevaluate your taste in football teams."

I tried to scowl, but a giggle escaped.

He moved closer to me, which caused a jolt to surge through my body.

"I'm sorry, Mr. Carson, but that won't be happening."

He continued to move closer to me. "We have plenty of time to work on it. I'm a very good leader."

Jack was standing a few inches away, and I fought hard to stop myself from wrapping my arms around him and kissing him. "Not to change the subject, but I don't think I would've made it through these past few days without you."'

A smile spread across his lips. "I'm glad it all worked out."

For some reason, I couldn't bring myself to leave his office. It felt like a magnetic force was pulling us together, and I was trying to fight against it. "I should go—"

Before I could finish my sentence, Jack's arms were around my hips and his lips were on mine. It was like my dream, only eighty thousand times better. I ran my hands through his hair as he kissed me with more power and urgency.

As wonderful as it was, I was torn between my attraction to him and thoughts of my career. The last thing I needed was more complications, so I pulled away and tried to catch my breath.

"I'm sorry," he said.

"No, don't apologize. That was—" I stopped talking before I said something I'd regret.

"Amazing? Exhilarating?" he offered.

I laughed. "Something like that."

He shrugged. "What's your opinion of me, Lexi?"

I folded my arms tightly against my chest. "I'm still trying to figure that out."

He raised his eyebrows. "Well, then, it's probably a good thing I'm going to be on this ship for a while."

I reached around him and grabbed the door handle. "Yes, it is." I touched my fingers to my lips and practically floated out of his office.

ABOUT THE AUTHOR

Melissa Baldwin is a planner-obsessed Disney fan who still watches Beverly Hills 90210 reruns and General Hospital.

She's a wife, mother, and journal keeper, who finally decided to write the book she talked about for years. She took her dream to the next level, and is now an award-winning, bestselling author of nineteen Romantic Comedy and Cozy Mystery novels and novellas. Melissa writes about charming, ambitious, and real women, and she considers these leading ladies to be part of her tribe.

When she isn't deep in the writing zone, this multitasking master organizer keeps busy by spending time with her family, chauffeuring her daughter, traveling, attempting yoga poses, and going on rides at Disney World.

To learn more about Melissa Baldwin, visit her online at:
www.authormelissabaldwin.com

Enjoyed this book? Check out these other novels in print now from Melissa Baldwin!

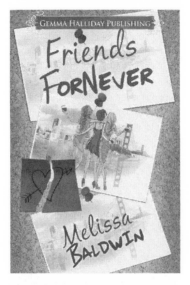

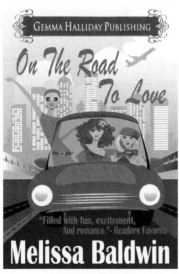

www.GemmaHallidayPublishing.com

Made in the USA
Middletown, DE
19 February 2022

61556213R00113